Less than Half an Hour Ago
She Had Found Him Despicable.

He pulled her from the rail and turned her around so that he could look at her. She felt the warmth of his fingers against her bare skin, an electric thrill darting through her at the intimate contact.

Neal's lips closed over hers in a kiss that was so gentle it brought an ache to her throat. Then, as the kiss lingered, the pressure increasing, the caress of Neal's hands running over her body—more and more demanding—she felt as though she would never again draw a full breath. When he lifted his lips from hers, his voice was like a sighing wind: "Jody, my Jody," he repeated. . . .

Dear Reader:

Silhouette Books is pleased to announce the creation of a new line of contemporary romances—*Silhouette Special Editions*. Each month we'll bring you six new love stories written by the best of today's authors—Janet Dailey, Brooke Hastings, Laura Hardy, Sondra Stanford, Linda Shaw, Patti Beckman, and many others.

Silhouette Special Editions are written with American women in mind; they are for readers who want more: more story, more details and descriptions, more realism, and more *romance. Special Editions* are longer than most contemporary romances allowing for a closer look at the relationship between hero and heroine with emphasis on heightened romantic tension and greater sensuous and sensual detail. If you want more from a romance, be sure to look for *Silhouette Special Editions* on sale this February wherever you buy books.

We welcome any suggestions or comments, and I invite you to write us at the address below.

Karen Solem
Editor-in-Chief
Silhouette Books
P.O. Box 769
New York, N. Y. 10019

JANE CONVERSE
Moonlit Path

Silhouette *Romance*
Published by Silhouette Books New York
America's Publisher of Contemporary Romance

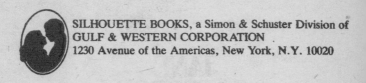

SILHOUETTE BOOKS, a Simon & Schuster Division of
GULF & WESTERN CORPORATION
1230 Avenue of the Americas, New York, N.Y. 10020

Copyright © 1982 by Silhouette Books, a Simon & Schuster
Division of Gulf & Western Corporation

Distributed by Pocket Books

ISBN: 0-671-57129-X

First Silhouette Books printing January, 1982

10 9 8 7 6 5 4 3 2 1

America's Publisher of Contemporary Romance

Printed in the U.S.A.

Moonlit
Path

Chapter One

Seated before the mirror of the built-in dressing table in her cabin, Jody Sommers held the blue-and-gold plastic pin up to her shoulder. Underneath her name, incredibly, were the words ASSISTANT CRUISE DIREC-TOR. Incredible, because she had applied for the job only last week, aware that she would have been more qualified to engineer a moon landing than to supervise the recreation of four hundred wealthy passengers aboard the luxurious *Caribe Queen*.

She had applied for the job to pacify her mother, who had seen the advertisement in a Miami newspaper. Jody had been a camp counselor, hadn't she? She had taught arts and crafts at a summer camp during her first and only year at college, hadn't she? It did no good to try to convince her mom that teaching ten-year-olds to make papier-mâché masks was not quite the same as keeping passengers aboard a luxury liner entertained. More an oversized yacht than one of the many commer-cial cruise ships plying the Caribbean, the *Queen* catered to a clientele that demanded, and got, the best in accommodations, cuisine, service and amusements.

Miraculously, after a brief interview with Preston MacCauley, a nervous, dapper, fiftyish man whose professional smile seemed as permanently affixed to his face as his silvery moustache, Jody had been hired. There had followed a hectic week of assembling a wardrobe. She had tried on the sportswear in the bedroom of her parents' little retirement cottage in

Sarasota, reasonably pleased with the result of a tightly budgeted shopping spree. The pale blue chiffon gown reflected the color of her eyes; the beige formal complemented her short, tousled, honey-colored hair. And the colorful sportswear had seemed exactly right for a Caribbean cruise until she had seen the passengers boarding at the Port of Miami's Dodge Island early today. Their departure clothing had obviously been purchased in one-of-a-kind boutiques that featured designer apparel. Even more dismaying was Jody's impression that the "brand-new look" was probably considered "gauche" among the women who could afford an extended vacation aboard the *Caribe Queen*. Pre-faded jeans seemed to be the "in" costume, clearly stating that this was hardly their first costly cruise.

Jody's momentary panic about her wardrobe emphasized her fears that she was not qualified to direct the activities of this idle rich crowd. And her boss, when asked what was expected of her, scurried off claiming that he was "busy, busy, busy" and would give her a briefing after the ship was at sea. "Explore the ship," Mr. MacCauley had said. "Meet me in the Nautilus Lounge before the first dinner seating." With a reminder that Jody was to call him "Prez," and that the ship's daily bulletin would answer many of her questions, he had left her in the small office from which the cruise director's activities were conducted.

Jody had taken the beautifully illustrated folder to her cabin. She learned that the Captain's Welcome Aboard dinner, shortly after they sailed, would be informal. There were descriptions of shore excursions of San Juan; their immediate destination was Puerto Rico. And the lavish midnight buffet would be served tonight, in the Aquamarine Lounge, next to the casino.

Studying the cruise ship's advertising brochure, with its drawings of decks and public rooms, Jody's mind whirled. The *Caribe Queen* was more than a floating hotel; it was a veritable city of shops, dining rooms, cabaret and disco rooms, huge salons and bars. How would she ever find her way around the ship, let alone pretend to be an expert who advised others?

Part of the cruise director's job was to give lectures describing the next port of call. How long would it take before Jody could help him with that assignment? She had never visited the romantic dots in the Caribbean that were included in the ship's itinerary. But how exciting it was to think of visiting islands she had only dreamed about; Curacao and Martinique, Tortola and St. Thomas! As the ship had pulled away from its moorings, with one of the three shipboard bands blaring, and as the Florida coastline had disappeared in a sunset blaze of salmon and slate and magenta streaks, Jody had watched from the observation deck just below the bridge, unable to believe that this was really happening to her.

Now, barely feeling the motion of the ship, Jody had set the bulletin aside, dressed in a new lime green shift, and found her hands trembling with excitement as she applied her makeup. Her apprehension was tempered by joy, almost laughing aloud as she reminded herself that too much lipstick would overemphasize her mouth, which she thought of as too large, and that her hands were too shaky to do a good job of lining her eyes.

Suddenly realizing that the first seating in the dining room was at six, and that it was nearly a quarter of, Jody hurried out of her cabin. A fine start, being late for her first meeting with Prez MacCauley! Given her lack of experience, it was a miracle that he had hired her in the first place; the least she could do was to be dependable.

Jody's cabin, along with those of most of the crew members, was on the lowermost deck. An elevator took her to the fourth level and into a maze of richly carpeted corridors, one of which, she hoped, would lead her to the Nautilus Lounge. She reached the end of one long passageway to see a sign pointing toward the place where she was to meet Prez. She had been going in the wrong direction. Really worried now about being late, Jody said aloud, "Ohh, *no!*" and made an abrupt turn to retrace her footsteps. And it happened! She collided with someone who had apparently been walking directly behind her.

Jody gasped at the impact and a sudden shower. She backed off hurriedly from a tall man who was holding a nearly empty highball glass, the contents of which had splashed over his light blue sport shirt. Jody froze, staring first at the huge wet splotch that darkened the pastel silk shirt, then at the glass, and, finally, in breathless embarrassment at the man's face. It was an incredibly handsome face, but the dark eyes regarded Jody with utter disgust. Before she could apologize, a deeply resonant voice, heavy with sarcasm, asked, "Do you always talk to yourself? And don't you signal when you brake for sudden stops?"

Jody averted the annoyed gaze, her eyes looking down at the scattering of ice cubes at her feet. "I'm sorry," she said. Her voice was barely above a whisper. "I'm so . . . you can't know . . . I'm so terribly sorry!"

She looked up again to see the stranger's black-lashed eyes regarding her with an expression that, strangely, combined boredom with females in general and with her in particular. Yet, even more strangely, there seemed to be a glint of interest, too. Never had a man looked at her with an expression that made her so totally aware of herself. She felt a rush of heat through her body, knowing that her face had probably turned scarlet. Nor had she ever, outside of movie magazines, looked at a more devastatingly attractive male. He simply stood there, looking at her, saying nothing.

Jody repeated her apology, stammering, "Your . . . drink. I'll . . . I'll have to get you another drink." She knew before the sentence was completed that she had made a foolish remark.

"Oh, I think I can manage a replacement myself,"

the man said. He sounded as chilly as the few ice cubes that still remained in his glass.

Jody nodded, feeling close to tears. "But your shirt! I don't know what to say except . . ."

"I brought an extra one along, just in case," the man said.

"You don't have to be nasty!" Jody flared. "I told you I was sorry. I'm supposed to be in the Nautilus Lounge meeting . . ."

"Meeting a man. And I seem to have gotten in your way."

His tone was thick with innuendo. But Jody wasn't going to explain to him that her appointment was with her boss, that she was nervous enough about being late, embarrassed enough about the accident, without having it rubbed into her. "If you can't accept an apology, like a gentleman, I . . . I guess there's nothing more I can say." She was trembling, both with anger at the man's officious bad manners and with the effect of his nearness. Even in the ludicrous wet shirt, he exuded a sex-charged maleness that left Jody weak. She was breathing hard, wishing she could appear as calm and in control of herself as this aggravating man.

He was examining the shirt now. It was plastered against a broad, muscular chest. "Ah, well. You've come up with a fairly original way to get acquainted with strangers," he said. This time, when he raised his glance to look at Jody, his expression was one of amusement—malicious amusement that fired Jody's anger with him.

"If you're implying that I . . . ran into you deliberately," Jody seethed, "you really flatter yourself. Someone as rude as you are . . . believe me, you're someone I'd much rather avoid!"

"In that case," the man said with exaggerated politeness, "you won't mind stepping aside so that I can go on to my suite?"

Jody's humiliation rose as she realized that she was

blocking his way in the narrow aisle. But before she could step aside, the man had reached out with his free hand, grasping her arm and moving her aside gently but firmly, handling her as though she were an inanimate object that just happened to be in his way. Though it seemed to Jody that he held his hand against her bare upper arm longer than was necessary.

"Perhaps we'll run into each other again before this cruise is over. I hope my supply of shirts holds out!" He smiled, showing even white teeth. It was a smile that he probably knew had an overwhelming effect upon women. Yet it was totally demeaning; he was all but laughing at her.

Jody's eyes welled with tears. She could think of nothing to say and stood numb and motionless as the man made his way down the corridor. Unable to move, she was frozen by more than her embarrassment, more than her fury. She could still feel the warm pressure of his hand against her flesh, the penetrating stare of dark eyes that smoldered with implications. No man had ever looked at her so intently before or left her more shaken.

She was still disturbed by the man's impact upon her as she hurried, gasping for breath, into the vast Nautilus Lounge.

Decorated in a sea green and gold seashell motif, the airy lounge afforded a spectacular view of the Caribbean from a glass wall. White leather settees and wide modern chairs were spaced for intimate conversations, many of them filled with passengers whose animation was no doubt related to the busy bar that flanked another side of the room. Jody looked around, spotting Prez MacCauley at a corner table, sitting alone with a tall, exotic, fruit-decorated drink before him.

She was apologizing again. "I'm sorry if I'm late," she said as Prez rose to greet her. "I . . . ran into someone."

The literal accurateness of the statement brought an

unexpected smile to Jody's face. She was pleased to see that her boss was not looking at his watch and glowering at her. On the contrary, in his immaculate white suit, he looked as though he were on vacation and had all the time in the world. "Running into people will be part of your job," he said amiably. He flashed his practiced, professional smile. *His* job, Jody remembered, was to keep everyone aboard happy.

Jody took the chair that Prez held out for her, shaking her head when Prez asked if she wanted a drink. "Not on the job," she said. "I'm having a hard enough time getting oriented without drinking."

Prez grinned. "Well, whatever. I have a few minutes I can call my own. I know I've neglected you, dear. Let's talk."

Jody nodded. "You haven't told me just what it is I'm supposed to be doing."

"True," Prez admitted. "True. Every cruise ship is different."

He had made it sound as though Jody had worked aboard other vacation ships. Had he forgotten that she had been honest with him when she told him that she had never been aboard a vessel larger than her uncle's rowboat when she was ten?

"Keep in mind that the C.Q. is light years ahead of any other ship cruising the Caribbean," Prez said. "We not only offer more luxurious accommodations and a higher crew-to-passenger ratio than any other ship going, but our cruise is more extended, covering more ports. Meaning, of course, that this is the most expensive Caribbean cruise vacation available. And our passengers expect nothing but the best."

Prez went on, telling Jody about the enormous crew and cruise staff that included stewards and maids, bartenders and croupiers, beauticians and entertainers. "Can you even begin to imagine how many chefs and waiters are involved?" Prez asked. He still hadn't told Jody what he expected of her. "We serve an early-bird breakfast next to both pools, a more elaborate breakfast at two sittings in the dining room, an elaborate mid-morning bouillon, luncheon alfresco or in the dining room, afternoon tea, spectacular dinners, midnight buffet. This alone keeps our passengers quite busy. So do shore excursions. In between, we see to it that there is not a moment of boredom."

Jody was told about Prez's duties, which included M.C.-ing the nightly cabaret shows, giving morning lectures on what the passengers could expect during shore trips, overseeing the special parties, bridge tournaments, dance and exercise classes, and seeing that the ship's game equipment and library were replenished after each cruise. He hired the entertainers, and saw to it that the bulletin of daily activities reached the print shop on time and was distributed to each room early in the morning. "In my copious free time," he quipped, "I have to plan ahead for seminars and special-interest groups. Come up with ideas for theme parties." He sipped nervously at his drink. "And you want to know how you can help?" he asked, finally recognizing Jody's need to know. "For openers, dear, I hope you have noticed that the female passengers aboard considerably outnumber the men."

Jody looked around the lounge. She hadn't noticed it earlier; most of the passengers she had seen boarding were middle-aged couples. But here in the lounge there were several groups of women.

"Women alone," Prez said. "Widows, divorcees. Some looking for a husband, some only wanting to get away and enjoy themselves. But enjoying is helped, especially on the dance floor, by male companions. Correct?"

"I suppose so," Jody acknowledged.

"Which brings me to one of the most important of your duties. An assistant cruise director is also a hostess. Although our ladies may not acquire lifetime mates or realize their romantic fantasies, I will expect you to see that while they are aboard the C.Q. they will have a smashing good time."

"I don't see how I . . ."

Jody's question was cut off. "You will see to it that every unattached male capable of creeping or crawling is present at every one of our social functions. At cocktail parties, dances, sports events, even Bingo games. With your fresh, attractive appearance and pleasant manner, I should think it will be easy for you to supplement our officers with those few single, unaccompanied men who are with us on this cruise. Do not, if you please, allow any member of my sex to seclude himself with a good book."

Prez laughed at his facetious remark and Jody was forced to smile. "I'll do my best," she promised.

"Of course you will." He went on talking for a while, telling Jody that he was quite aware of her lack of experience and explaining, "My previous assistant, you see, eloped with one of the musicians, virtually jumping ship on our return to Miami, giving me no notice whatsoever. I trust you will not do likewise, Jody." Prez stared at the rim of his glass for a moment. His eyes, which reflected a peculiar yellow cast, narrowed. "I suppose I should have asked this earlier. Are you aboard because you're recovering from a broken heart? Or simply in hopes of finding a wealthy husband?"

"Neither," Jody told him firmly. She didn't feel disposed to tell Prez that the closest she had come to having her heart broken was an abortive summer romance with another camp counselor. It couldn't have been real love, she had decided later; her recovery had been too swift. Since then, she had enjoyed a few casual dates, but all of her romances had been daydreams. No one had materialized to shower her with kisses, nor had she met anyone who made her want to be kissed. She yearned, as every young woman does, for words of affection, for declarations of love, for strong, protective arms holding her close while the man of her dreams whispered, "I love you." But that dream man was exactly that; perhaps, considering her high expectations, he didn't even exist. "Neither," Jody repeated. "I needed a job. And this one is . . . fantastic."

Prez nodded his approval, smoothed his silver moustache and went on to tell Jody that her duties would include special events for the seminar groups that were usually part of the passenger list on every cruise. "Doctors, golfers, lodge members—all sorts of groups with specialized interests. They usually have their own program, which we try to supplement. Certainly we see to it that they have privacy for their meetings and private parties. However, we *do* try to integrate them with our other passengers. The two special groups we have aboard for this cruise will be a good beginning for you."

Jody was told that the passenger list included a large group of arts and crafts teachers and a special seminar of distinguished attorneys. "The first group is almost one hundred percent female," Prez said. "The lawyers . . . most have brought their wives." He made a quick grimace. "Or reasonable facsimiles thereof. We are very discreet. However, there are several attorneys aboard who are unattached, at least so far as this cruise is concerned. One," Prez said slowly, "is about to join us."

Jody followed Prez's gesture and the direction of his gaze. She caught her breath. The tall man, whose stride was followed by the eyes of every woman in the room, was someone she had met before. He had changed the blue silk shirt for a beige linen, embroidered in brown at the collar. The shirt was unbuttoned halfway down, exposing his tanned, powerful chest. And it was not only his handsomeness that commanded attention; as he made his way toward a table near the wide expanse of glass, his walk was poised and sure, as though he

16

were in command of the room, though he seemed unaware of anyone else in it. He wasn't carrying a glass this time; in one hand he held a black looseleaf notebook.

"Jody? Hello, hello?"

Jody released her breath, aware that Prez had noticed her sudden discomfiture. She returned her attention to Prez. "I'm sorry. I was just . . ."

"Looking as though you'd seen a ghost," Prez finished.

"Not a ghost. Just . . ." She fought against sounding like a flustered schoolgirl, faking a quick laugh. "Just someone I've . . . I've run into before."

"Well, I want you to run into him again," Prez said. "And see to it that he is introduced to everyone around."

Jody gulped. "But I don't know any of these . . ."

"You'll let them introduce themselves. You'll simply serve as a catalyst. And, more important, you will make certain that Mr. Rainey is urged to attend the captain's after-dinner dance tonight."

Jody was beginning to feel queasy. Walk up to that sneering, unsympathetic . . .?

"You were just asking where I need help," Prez said pointedly. He must have noticed Jody's reluctant expression. "This is where."

"You . . . mentioned his name," Jody said.

"Surely I don't have to *tell* you his name?" Prez looked astounded. "Neal Rainey? The . . . probably the best-known trial lawyer in the United States?"

Jody's feeling of inadequacy began to return. "I . . . don't know *any* lawyers, Mr. MacCauley. No one's ever sued me."

Prez made a sound of utter disbelief. "But you've heard him on television talk shows? You know about his best-selling book?"

She felt more than ever like a country bumpkin,

thoroughly out of place in this sophisticated setting. She had to admit that she hadn't heard of Mr. Rainey's book, either.

Prez was pleasant, as always. Trained to make people feel comfortable, he said, "Well, that may be an advantage. You'll be more at ease with the man if you aren't too impressed." He rose suddenly. "The attorneys don't have anything scheduled until Rainey's keynote speech tomorrow morning. Can you imagine what his presence will add to our gala tonight? The ladies will think they've died and gone to heaven. Go over and talk to him, Jody. Your first assignment." Prez flashed an impish grin. "I'm sure he'll be delighted. He looks positively morose."

Prez announced that he had an appointment with the purser and hurried off, leaving his half-finished drink on the table. But, in spite of his friendly manner, he had made it clear that he expected Jody to do what he had asked her to do. She had been hired because he had been desperate; unqualified, she would be expected to prove her worth on this first cruise. Prez's parting smile had been . . . yes, it had been *challenging*.

Jody sat rigidly at the table as the cruise director left the lounge, waving cheerfully at everyone he passed. She wished that she had let Prez order a drink for her; maybe a few sips would have given her courage.

There was no doubt about it, she was on trial. Jody stole a quick glance at the man who had unsettled her earlier. He had opened his notebook and was concentrating on its contents. Jody took in the sight of expertly styled, almost blue-black wavy hair, a strongly rugged face, tanned at the beginning of a cruise; he must enjoy outdoor activities, she thought, for he certainly didn't have a courtroom pallor. As he turned his head, he displayed a cleanly chiseled profile with a strong, clefted chin. His downcast eyes were framed by heavy black brows that turned up slightly at the ends to give him an attractive but disturbing devilish appearance.

He had treated her abominably. It would have been difficult enough to walk up to *any* strange man. Under the circumstances, the effort filled Jody with dread.

Should she walk over to the bar, ask the bartender what Mr. Rainey drank, carry a replacement for the one she had spilled to the lawyer's table? No, that might only annoy him. If he wanted a drink, he had only to hail a passing waiter or cocktail waitress. Jody swallowed hard and got to her feet.

Crossing the lounge, she gained confidence by smiling at some of the other passengers. Most were middle-aged ladies in flamboyantly-colored resort frocks. Some were with portly, drink-sipping men, others were alone. All of them returned Jody's smile. This was her *job,* for heaven's sake! Smile, greet people, make them feel at home aboard the ship. Squaring her shoulders as she approached his table, Jody told herself that Mr. Rainey was no more or less important than any of the other people in the lounge.

If Neal Rainey was aware of Jody's approach, he pretended not to be. He kept his eyes riveted on the pages in his large notebook.

By the time she had reached his table near the glass wall, Jody was wishing the Nautilus Lounge would open up and swallow her. What could she say to him? She made a determined effort to sound sprightly and hostess-like. "Hello. I hope you've forgiven me for being so awkward. I'm Jody Sommers."

Neal Rainey lifted his dark eyes from his papers slowly. He looked as if she had just arrived from Mars; some strange creature who had arrived on earth with the sole purpose of disturbing him, not just once, but now again. At the same time, the heavy-lidded eyes exuded a virility, a magnetism, that reduced Jody to breathlessness once more.

There was a long silence, adding to Jody's discomfort. Then, in a subdued, disinterested tone, she heard him say, "If I assure you that your apology is accepted, can I expect you to respect my privacy?"

She felt the warm rush of blood to her face. "Of course. I . . . I didn't mean to . . ." She felt too confused to go on.

"Please understand that if I didn't want to be alone, I have any number of friends aboard to keep me company." He nodded politely and resumed his reading.

Jody stood beside the table, feeling more awkward than ever before in her life. He had made her feel cheap and miserable. Why? What was wrong with him? Didn't people take vacation cruises to meet other people, to make new friends, to socialize? She had been coldly dismissed, like a . . . a hustling bar girl! Something inside her wanted her to run, but something else demanded that she explain to this insufferably rude snob that she was not attracted by his probable wealth, his prestige, his almost theatrical good looks, and certainly not his boorish manners. "This wasn't my idea," she said. "Prez MacCauley asked me to . . . since you're on board without . . . without your wife or . . ."

Hopeless! She had made the situation even worse, imagining her garbled, easily misinterpreted words through the ears of an aloof stranger. She made one more desperate attempt to clarify why she had come to the man's table uninvited. "Prez didn't want you to spend this evening alone."

Her face was on fire, though it was being stared at by an iceberg. "I don't happen to know anyone named Mr. MacCauley." The words were precisely articulated, with all the sharpness of a razor's edge. "I don't know how he, or you, determined that I am aboard this ship without a female to accompany me, though I can well guess." He remained seated, but the attorney seemed to be towering over Jody, looking down at her with undisguised contempt. "But may I assure you, Miss . . . whatever your name is, that when you interrupted me, I was studying a speech that I'm to give before my colleagues tomorrow morning. If I spend this evening alone, please tell Mr. MacCauley that it will be by choice. And if I decide to have companionship, it will be of my own choosing."

Jody's humiliation threatened to destroy her. Only giving free expression to her anger would save her the added embarrassment of bursting into tears and running from the room. "I told you this wasn't my idea," she said. Her voice wavered, but she went on. "I'm . . . new on this ship. Prez insisted that I . . . come over and talk to you about tonight. He's . . . he's my boss."

A faintly amused expression crossed Neal Rainey's handsome face. He almost purred his response. "Really. How very candid of you."

It took Jody a few moments to realize his implication; her boss was in the business of sending young women to solicit the attention of lone males aboard ship! What kind of mind would jump to that conclusion? A blinding rage seized Jody. "Do you always think about people in the worst . . . the sleaziest, most demeaning . . ." She gasped for breath. "Do you always enjoy making people feel . . . miserable?"

"Or uncomfortable? I was about to ask the same question of you." Mr. Rainey had fixed her with a dark, uncompromising stare. He might have had a shaky witness pinned on the stand, boring the person with his eyes, reducing his prey to jelly. "Look, while I didn't enjoy being drenched with Scotch and water, I'm willing to dismiss that as an accident. But being approached by a strange woman, especially when it's quite obvious that I'm preoccupied, doesn't require that I be polite. Kindly pass that word along to . . . whatever you said his name is . . . your 'boss.' And also tell him that if I'm solicited again, I'll have a word with the captain and see that you're both removed from this ship at the next port!"

Jody sucked in an audible breath of air. If he had used the word "procurer" instead of "boss," the lawyer's meaning could not have been more clear. She no longer cared about this "dream job" that placed such cheapening demands upon her. She hated Prez for insisting that she talk to this vicious man; she despised Neal Rainey more than she had ever despised another human being on earth. "How can you be so vile to someone who's only doing her job? I'm new on this ship and . . ."

"So I've gathered," the lawyer said. His bright, knowing smile left Jody limp with fury.

"You . . ." Jody shook her head back and forth, searching for scathing words. "You're the most arrogant, unfeeling, conceited, rude . . ."

"Detestable," he said quietly. He returned his attention to his speech notes. "You forgot to say 'detestable.'"

"I hadn't come to that yet," Jody cried. Her voice had risen to a shrill pitch. Several people at a nearby table turned to stare at her briefly, then, politely, turned away. As she started to leave, Neal Rainey looked up to stare at her, too, his eyes sweeping over Jody in a head-to-toe examination that was half-derisive, half-approving. Then he gave her a patronizing nod that said she was dismissed.

Jody could only turn and hurry out of the lounge. She wanted to scream, to cry, to tell everyone aboard that she didn't want this . . . this exercise in abasement that passed for a job. Most of all, she wanted to find a haven where she could be alone.

It was the worst possible beginning, Jody thought. Would Prez understand if she told him that the celebrated attorney was the most insulting person she had ever met? Or was she expected to handle situations like this with tact and diplomacy? She didn't care.

There was almost no one on the glassed-in observation deck. Jody thought of sinking into a deck chair, letting her tears come, deciding what to do about the encounter with Neal Rainey. But she discovered that she was not alone. A couple, probably in their early fifties, came walking past her toward the stern. The man was sandy-haired, balding and paunchy. A loud magenta leisure suit contrasted with the woman's emerald green satin cocktail dress. The woman looked exasperated and a bit exhausted, listening to the man say reproachfully, "If you're any kind of a mother, Elise, you'll stop hounding her and let her have a good time. That's why we came, isn't it? For all of us to have a good time?"

Noticing Jody, the man gave her a meaningful look that said she was intruding upon a family argument. Jody left the observation area and made her way to the elevators.

Prez would probably have other things for her to do this evening. She would have to observe, at least, what went on during the captain's first-night-at-sea dinner and the dance that was scheduled to follow. If she stayed busy, she would put Neal Raincy out of her mind. He was probably the only nasty-tempered passenger on board and it would be ironic to let him spoil this dream cruise, this perfect job. Jody decided to return to her cabin, freshen up, and then check in with Prez.

She was crammed into one of the elevators with a merry group of women when one of them smiled at her shyly and said, "Isn't this fun? Is this your first cruise?"

She was supposed to be an assistant to the cruise director; would an honest reply reveal that the *Caribe Queen* hired green personnel to give advice to its passengers? Jody was saved from having to respond when one of the other women said, "Oh, you must not be with our group. You aren't wearing one of our pins."

She was making a reference, Jody realized, to the

large crepe paper-trimmed badges that everyone else in the elevator wore at her shoulder. Trimmed with chenille pipe cleaners spiraled to look like green ivy stems, each of the rose-pink flower-shaped ID pins had a white circle in the center, bearing its wearer's name and home town. This was obviously the arts and crafts group. Mention of identification pins sent Jody's hand instinctively up to her shoulder. A sinking feeling came over her. Her pin! The pin that identified her as assistant cruise director! In her haste to meet Prez, she had left it on her dresser. And even Prez hadn't noticed that she wasn't wearing the pin that would have identified her to everyone on board as an employee!

Would Neal Rainey have treated her with respect if he had known that she was not soliciting his patronage? No. Certainly he was intelligent enough, perceptive enough, to know that she didn't look or behave like a shipboard prostitute. He had to know that such an activity would never be tolerated aboard ship. Rainey was an incredibly rude egomaniac, impressed with his own success and physical attractions. There was no excuse for the way he had behaved.

Still, as she readied herself for the first-night-out activities, this time remembering her ID pin, Jody found her thoughts returning to the handsome attorney, even though she was annoyed with herself for letting him have such a strong effect upon her. She wanted to forget that, along with his disparaging remarks and baleful looks, he had gotten a bright glint in his eyes when he had let them sweep over her. Just remembering that look sent an unfamiliar shudder through Jody. She felt warm, flushed with the remembrance, her body reacting in a way she had never known it to react before.

Brushing her honey-colored hair, she looked at herself closely in the mirror. Did he think she was attractive? Not really beautiful; she didn't have classic features (*he* did!) and her nose was slightly upturned, her heart-shaped face more elfin than exotic. But had he thought she was, at least, passably pretty?

Jody slammed the hairbrush down on the dresser, furious with herself. Why was she even thinking about the man? In the next instant she was projecting herself to another time, another place, other circumstances. She imagined their meeting pleasant, their attraction for each other immediate and irresistible. In this fleeting daydream Neal Rainey was gracious and even gallant.

Insane! Ridiculous, childish and insane! Jody sprang up from the vanity bench. Next thing she knew, her wild, romantic imagination would have her on the deck with a full moon overhead. His strong arms would be drawing her close, his lips would press against hers and then he would whisper, "I adore you, Jody. I've fallen madly in love with you!"

Jody concentrated on the man's actual words. It was the best cure for her immature habit of letting silly romantic daydreams take possession of her mind. Remember how he had acted, remember what he had said! Stay furious with him! And if you're lucky, Jody told herself, you won't see Mr. Rainey during the rest of this cruise, which is the same as saying you'll never see the despicable creature again.

Chapter Two

Jody saw Neal Rainey again sooner than she had expected. And if there had been any doubt about his importance, it was erased by his presence at the captain's table. Resplendent in his white, gold braid-trimmed uniform, Captain Di Marro was playing host to seven other people. His guests would be different each night, Jody knew, but the first night was reserved for the most prestigious passengers aboard the *Caribe Queen*. Neal Rainey's already rapacious ego was being well fed tonight!

Jody gave her attention to the lesser lights with whom she had been seated. While most of the personnel took their meals in the crew and cruise staff dining room, Prez had arranged for Jody to dine with the passengers where she could practice the art of being his hostess-assistant. Here Jody was thrilled by the veritable army of white-coated waiters, the elegantly printed and extensive gourmet menu, the crystal stemware and gleaming silver. Arrangements of red roses dominated each linen covered table and an unobtrusive maître d' saw to it that the music of a string quartet was not too loud to drown out the jovial conversations.

It seemed, however, that the conversation at one end of Jody's table was strained. Elise and Dalton West-brook, whom Jody recognized as the couple she had seen earlier on the observation deck, seemed to be at odds. Their talk was mostly between themselves, with occasional comments by a stunning young blonde who had been introduced as their daughter, Diane. Still in her teens, the girl wore a tightly fitted white cocktail dress that contrasted dramatically with her tanned face and arms. Apparently her behavior was the subject of her parents' tense dialog. Diane ignored them both, making a production number of ordering *Coquilles St. Jacques* as an appetizer and lobster thermidor as her entrée, then making critical remarks about the wine list. Jody got the impression that the girl, whose apple-green eyes had been inherited from her mother, was Mr. Westbrook's pet. Elise Westbrook had apparently found some fault with Diane's actions, for Diane's father was heard saying, "She's young. Don't let's keep bringing up the past. Let's have *fun.*"

Politely trying to avoid overhearing the Westbrooks' family matters, three women who introduced themselves as Janice, Eunice and Virginia, all three from El Centro, California, chatted excitedly about how they would spend their time in San Juan. Jody was occupied by a pleasantly round-faced fortyish man with cornflower blue eyes. He was Terry Allin, M.D., Jody learned. By contrast with Neal Raincy, he made her feel completely at ease in this opulent, unfamiliar setting. By the time their blazing rum-flavored Baked Alaskas were served, Jody felt comfortable enough with the ship's doctor to tell him about her unpleasant encounter with one of the ship's passengers.

"I wasn't wearing my name pin at the time," Jody added. "Do you think he really thought I was . . . you know . . . trying to pick him up?"

"One look at you should have told him otherwise," the doctor said. "I suppose he's wary. He has problems."

Jody glanced quickly toward the captain's table, then back to her dinner companion. *"That* man has problems? He's supposed to be tops in his field. Wealthy, no doubt. Best-selling author, Prez tells me." Jody didn't have to comment on Neal Rainey's appearance; that was too obvious to mention.

Dr. Allin smiled, somewhat wistfully, Jody thought. "None of us are immune from problems, Jody. The cruise staff grapevine has it that he was about to be married to some glamorous socialite in San Francisco. That's his home, you know. He was out of town for about four months prior to the wedding date. Some bizarre murder case, I believe. Anyway, almost on the eve of the wedding, he learned that while he was away doing his thing, his lady-love had been doing hers. With some young rock star."

"And, of course he couldn't forgive her," Jody said. "It took three apologies before he forgave me just for dousing him with a little Scotch and water."

"I don't know the details. In his book, he talks about playing the field. I gather he's an embittered man. Maybe not a misogynist . . ."

"A what?"

"A woman-hater," the doctor explained. "But certainly wary of serious entanglements. Once is enough to be made a fool of—humiliated before your friends and, in his case, before the public."

"It happened to me once," Jody confided. "The worst part was having to admit to my friends that I'd been dropped."

The round blue eyes examined Jody's face. "Someone you cared about dropped *you?* I presume he's institutionalized. An obvious mental case."

Jody laughed at the compliment. Terry Allin had a warmth and sincerity that were almost boyish, in spite of his professional stature. "You mentioned Mr. Rainey's book. I'm beginning to think I'm the only person on earth who hasn't even heard of it, let alone read it."

"It's called *A Life on the Line.* Autobiographical. And very interesting," Jody was told. The doctor seemed unwilling to dwell on Neal Rainey. He reverted back to Jody and her broken romance. "Are you aboard to get away from the scene of your heartbreak?" His blue eyes twinkled.

"Oh, that was a long time ago," Jody said.

"Ages ago," he mocked playfully. "You can't be more than twenty."

"Twenty-two," Jody said. "And very naive, and totally untraveled. And scared to death someone will ask me what to wear for some certain activity, or what to see in Martinique, or what wine to drink with . . . some French Whatever I've never tasted in my life."

"Answers," the doctor said, his eyes admiring Jody's honesty. "Tell them to wear whatever they think will look best. On Martinique, the excursion will automatically take them to the volcanic ruins of St. Pierre. And we have a wine steward to tell them what to drink with French Whatever." The doctor patted Jody's hand, a touch that lingered just a moment too long to be completely paternal. "Just be as charming and pretty and friendly as you are, Jody. You'll be the best assistant cruise director we've ever had aboard."

Jody thanked the doctor, and after he had offered to acquaint her with the ship's ports of call whenever he was free, Terry Allin turned his attention to the three women from California. They were all physical therapists, in their late forties or early fifties, and they were not the typical wealthy cruise ship passengers. They admitted that they had been saving for years to find out how the upper crust lives, and the doctor went out of his way to be exceptionally charming and attentive. Jody liked his sensitivity. He knew that loneliness and isolation from the crowd can darken a long anticipated vacation. He all but ignored Jody until the end of the dinner, but instead of feeling snubbed, she felt a growing admiration for Dr. Allin.

While they were sipping their after-dinner liqueurs, Dalton Westbrook said, "We can fix *that* up, honey."

He was addressing his beautiful daughter. Then he called out across the table to Jody. "You can arrange that, can't you, miss?"

"Arrange what?" Jody asked.

"For my little girl here to be transferred to another table? It's not that she doesn't like our company, but you know how it is. The wife and I don't agree, but my feeling is Diane would have more fun if she wasn't stuck with family, know what I mean? Maybe set her up with some younger people."

Mrs. Westbrook sat tight-lipped and disapproving. She and her husband had both been drinking throughout the meal. Now it was apparent that Dalton Westbrook was making the request against her wishes.

"Whatever it takes, you just say the word," Mr. Westbrook went on. "Money's no object. Not where my little girl's concerned."

"Isn't he a doll?" Diane cooed. She and her father looked at each other fondly. Elise looked as though she could strangle them both.

"There's no charge involved," Jody said. "And you don't talk to me, you talk to the maître d'."

Jody felt a surge of pity for the henna-haired woman in the green satin gown. Instinct told her that Elise Westbrook was trying to be a sensible parent but was being overruled by a doting father. Their family squabble had cast a pall over the dinner table and Jody was relieved when Dr. Allin excused himself and got to his feet. "Sorry, folks, but I've got to get back to my office. First night out, meaning there will be more cases of *mal de mer* than the nurses can handle."

Jody stood up, too. "How can anyone get seasick? If I didn't know better, I'd think we're in a hotel dining room."

"Yes, the *C.Q.* has the last word in stabilizers," the doctor said. "But some people would feel queasy if you told them their three-story house was a boat."

Everyone laughed, and Jody went in search of Prez MacCauley. As she was leaving the dining room, she noticed that Neal Rainey was no longer at the captain's table. Would she see him later, at the dance, she wondered? Then, annoyed with herself for letting the question even occur to her, she managed to get lost twice before she found Prez in his office and got her assignment for the evening. She was to see that "there were no more wallflowers than necessary" in the ballroom.

Under glittering-colored lights, and to the strains of a versatile band that played everything from the last word in rock music to nostalgic "golden oldies," Jody found herself enjoying the process of encouraging passengers to mingle. She overcame a natural shyness and discovered that her identification pin gave her a certain degree of glamour and authority. If she could get through this cruise, by the next time the *C.Q.* sailed, she would actually be able to advise a new group of passengers on what to do, what to see in port, how to make the most of their time aboard ship.

Jody declined invitations to dance, seeing, instead, that the unescorted women had partners. She didn't have to perform this service for Diane Westbrook. The lovely blonde was easily the belle of the ball, enjoying her freedom from parents who drank, disagreed and bickered a little too much. Jody was surprised when, during a break in the music, the girl separated herself from one of the ship's officers and walked directly to the spot where Jody stood watching the festivities.

Diane flashed her dazzling smile. "I hope you didn't mind Daddy asking you to do the maître d's job," she said. "He's got a heart of gold, but the poor dear's been so busy making money, he hasn't gotten around too much."

"It's quite all right," Jody assured her.

"But he does understand that I can't have fun stuck

with a lot of old fogies three times a day. Mother would have me in a geriatrics home if she had her way. Or a convent."

Jody smiled. She hadn't liked Diane during dinner, finding her snobbish and even bratty, but now she sensed that this was just a facade. "Have you made arrangements to have your meals at a . . . livelier table?"

"No. I was hoping you'd do it for me." Diane's green eyes, heavily shadowed and mascaraed, took on an innocent little-girl look that Jody suspected was used whenever she wanted something. "You see, I . . . don't want just *any* table. And Mother would have a fit—maybe Daddy wouldn't even like it. But . . ." Diane dropped her voice to a throaty half-whisper. "There's an attorney on board. He sat at the captain's table tonight, but he won't be there tomorrow, will he?"

An uncomfortable fluttering had started in Jody's mid-section. "No. No, I don't imagine he will."

"Well, wherever they seat *him,* that's where I'd like to be." This time Diane's smile was dazzling. But a hard glint had come into her eyes, an expression that said she was accustomed to getting her way. "His name is Rainey. Neal Rainey. I found out that much about him. And I know he's mad about tennis. I *overheard* that. My kind of people, you know?"

"Mr. Rainey's on board with a large group," Jody said. "I imagine he'll be having his meals with other attorneys in his party."

"Please try," Diane said evenly. She sounded just short of having delivered an imperious command. But then there was that brilliant smile again, and as the music started up once more, Diane let herself be whirled onto the dance floor by the ship's purser, easily the most attractive man around.

Several times, Jody noticed that Diane appeared distracted, darting glances toward the wide entryway to the ballroom. She danced with a series of men, but she seemed hardly aware of them. Was she waiting for, hoping for someone to make an entrance? The attorney who was "her kind of people"?

No, I'm projecting, Jody decided. She had been watching the ballroom entrance herself, wondering if Neal Rainey would make an appearance. But, *why?* She was still infuriated by the man's attitude toward her. Why would she be disappointed because he hadn't come to the dance?

By one thirty the older people had drifted off to their cabins and suites and the younger crowd moved to the Castaways Club where flashing strobe lights and thumping disco music would keep going until dawn. Jody felt superfluous there and not a little tired from her long day.

There was an interminable wait for the elevator. On a sudden impulse, Jody decided to spend a few minutes on the sun deck at the stern. She had spent the entire evening in crowded rooms, almost totally unaware that she was aboard a ship. Terry Allin had been right about the *Caribe Queen*'s stabilizers; she could walk easily in her high-heeled pumps, feeling no motion under her feet at all.

During the day she had caught a glimpse of the glass-domed sun deck. Then it had been crowded with newly-boarded passengers who were making an exploration of the ship. Now the huge area looked deserted and gloomy, the pool drained to be refilled again in the morning, and the hundreds of deck chairs stretching emptily in the dim electric light. Jody kept walking toward the stern, stirred by the strangeness of the scene and the promise of seeing her first palm-studded island tomorrow.

Reaching the section that was not covered by the enormous transparent dome, Jody rested her folded arms on the rail. The sea, far below her, was dark. A soft breeze, unbelievably balmy, caressed her face. For

33

the first time since the *Caribe Queen* had pulled anchor, Jody felt that her girlhood dreams of sailing the Caribbean had really come true.

Millions of stars glittered against the velvet blackness of the sky. And the moon! Just a night or two short of being full, the moon was so enormous and golden and close that Jody thought she had stepped into a dream world. But it was not only that awesome satellite that made Jody hold her breath; it was the wide, silver-gold swath of light that the moon cast over the black water like some ethereal path, a shimmering road on which strange sea creatures or seafarers from ages long past might be seen walking.

Jody was drinking the eerie-beautiful sight with her eyes, positive that she would never again see anything to compare with this sight, when she was startled by a sound behind her. She gasped. She was certain that she was alone. And although she knew that she had nothing to fear, Jody's heart was racing from the shock as she heard someone say, "Doesn't seem quite real, does it?"

The deep masculine voice had a familiar ring. As Jody spun around, she knew in an instant why. His perfect features made almost spectral by the reflected moonglow, his eyes darker than she had remembered them, and somehow tinged with a sadness that did not go with his radiant smile, Neal Rainey was beside her near the rail.

When she regained her breath, Jody agreed. No, the awesome sight didn't belong to reality. But, then, neither did the sudden presence of this unbelievably handsome man. She had walked away from him in anger twice this evening. Why was she so stirred by his nearness now?

"Moonlit paths are all illusions," Jody heard him say. His voice had a distant, poetic quality. He might have been addressing the words to himself.

Jody was entranced, yet she made a determined

34

effort to sound icy. "Whatever that might mean," she said. The words sounded properly harsh.

"Am I disturbing you?" Neal Rainey asked. "If you'd rather be here alone . . ."

"I should have asked you the same question in the lounge this evening," Jody said.

"Touché, Miss Sommers."

"Well, it's true. People don't just come . . . barging up to other people and . . ."

He had placed his hands on the railing. Now he lifted them, turning slightly as though he were going to leave. A sudden desire to have him stay tempered Jody's chilliness. "Of course, I . . . I wasn't wearing my ID pin. You couldn't have known that I'm the new assistant cruise director." Jody hesitated, puzzled. "You know my name."

She looked up to see Neal Rainey nod once. Then the dim light revealed a warm, lopsided grin. "I met Mr. MacCauley. And I made it a point to ask."

"Oh." His change in manner was confusing. "Then you know I'm not just some . . . just some . . ."

"I should have known that when I saw how upset you were. Ladies of the evening don't get tears in their eyes when they're brushed off."

Jody had told him this before, but she repeated the words now. "It wasn't my idea. Walking up to you like that . . . if this wasn't my first day on the job, a job I'm just getting accustomed to. I told Prez I just couldn't walk up to a strange man and . . . try to tell him how he should spend his evening."

"No one has ever told me how to spend an evening," Neal Rainey said. For a moment Jody thought he was going to revert to his earlier, insulting style. But he added, "I owe you an apology. Please accept it, Jody."

He knew her first name, too. It was a trivial matter, but somehow Jody found it exhilarating. "I couldn't imagine anyone being as frosty as you were. Are you always that mean, or were you just in a bad mood, Mr. Rainey?"

"Irascible mood," he admitted. "From the time I got on board, I'd had it with this . . . floating singles bar. You'd think this shipload of man-hunters would be a little more subtle. When you came along, I had just freed myself from two of the most obnoxious, persistent . . ."

"Women," Jody finished. She became curt again. "But what an ego trip it must be! Having to brush off all those females who've fallen madly in love with you at first sight."

"Now who's being nasty?"

"I'm only commenting on what I just heard. Now that I know you aren't very fond of people, especially female people, I'll try to see to it that you're left alone. Certainly *I* won't trouble you again."

"I don't think you understand. I was trying to work on my speech for tomorrow. Today, actually. It must be past two A.M."

Jody remained silent. He could be egotistical and irritating, but his closeness filled her with an indescribable excitement. She could hardly believe that she was here in this fantastic setting talking with a man as attractive and intriguing as Neal Rainey. Yet some perverse instinct kept the sarcasm in her voice. "I think I do understand, Mr. Rainey. You wanted to work and . . ." Jody faked a breathless passion. "And we overwhelmed females simply wouldn't leave you alone."

He laughed shortly. "You'd think I'm the most conceited idiot alive if I told you that you're right. I hadn't gotten much sleep the past two nights, finishing up last-minute details with clients so that I could get away. And I really wanted my talk to make sense. I'm addressing people I stand in awe of and, frankly, if I was edgy, it's because I don't want to make a fool of myself tomorrow."

36

Amazing! He had self doubts. He was human, after all. Her tone softening, Jody said, "I told you your apology is accepted, Mr. Rainey."

"Neal," he said pointedly. "Neal. We're on vacation. Everybody on board seems to be on a first-name basis."

"I'm not on vacation," Jody reminded him.

They were silent for a while, staring at the wondrous sight before them. It seemed almost a sacrilege to speak. But though they exchanged no words, Jody felt a flow of communication between herself and the man who stood at the rail next to her, so close now that his forearm brushed against hers. If he was aware of the contact, Neal didn't move away from it.

Quietly, Neal asked, "Is this your deck, too, Jody?"

She smiled. "You've got to know better than that. This deck has exactly six suites, reserved for the *really* rich. I'm on what's called the Whitecap Deck. Bottom layer. Neat little cubicles occupied by the personnel."

"Doesn't matter. How much time does one spend in one's cabin? I, for one, intend to soak up the sun, see as much as I can of the islands, enjoy what I can of the seminar, play some tennis. Do you play?"

"'Fraid not." Jody regretted her answer. Somewhere in her subconscious she heard Diane Westbrook calling Neal Rainey "her kind of people" because they shared a love for tennis. Gorgeous young Diane who was already maneuvering to be seated at Neal's table. Jody's surge of jealousy made no sense to her. It was an emotion as unfamiliar and unreal as the moonlit path on the Caribbean. Yet, like the moonlit path, it was there. "'Fraid not," she repeated. "And, anyway, I'm on board to work, not to play."

"But, surely you'll get to see the islands? You'll have to, if you're going to be assisting the cruise director."

"Oh, I'm sure I will." Jody released a sigh. "I still can't believe I'm going to see all those beautiful places.

Aruba and Tortola may be old hat to you, but I couldn't have begun to afford to visit them. Not like you."

"I haven't been able to afford Aruba and Tortola, either," Neal said.

Jody turned to him in surprise. "Really?" she mocked.

"The time, Jody. I told myself for years that I couldn't afford the time. First, getting my degree, passing the bar, determined not to lean on the family name or prestige or money." A thin edge of bitterness crept into Neal's tone. "Oh, I was too busy to enjoy life. I was ambitious. Driven. Maybe I should have taken the time for fun. For people."

Was he berating himself because his work had taken him away from the woman he loved? Had he lost her through neglect? Jody didn't let Neal know that his broken romance was the subject of shipboard gossip. And when Neal said that he should have taken the time for "people," did he mean that he had made a mistake in investing his emotions in only one person? He was silent, his handsome profile set in grim lines while Jody waited for him to go on. When he didn't, she said, "This is a first for you, too, then?"

"Yes. First vacation in more years than I can remember."

A lone, small cloud appeared out of nowhere, it seemed, drifting across the face of the yellow moon for a few seconds, obscuring its light and erasing the path of moonlight on the sea. Then the cloud passed and the iridescent road was before them again. Jody sensed a strong rapport undulating between them, which added to the dreamlike quality of the scene. What was she doing here in this heavenly place, listening to the confidences of the most attractive, puzzling man she had ever met?

And Neal *was* pouring out confidences, suddenly, although he spoke in a distant tone that implied he might have been talking to himself. "Yes, I've been so preoccupied with getting ahead. I remember when I got involved with writing my book. I was in a courtroom all day, then pounding a typewriter half the night, sometimes all night long. I didn't write it with any hope of becoming a best-selling writer. I had no idea the book would take off the way it did . . . that so many people would want to know about the life of a trial lawyer. But while I was wrapped up in that project, I wouldn't have thought of taking a vacation. And, during that period, I know I was . . . neglecting certain people."

"One in particular?" Jody couldn't help asking the question, though she wished immediately afterward that she hadn't.

She couldn't see his face too clearly, but Jody sensed the long searching look that Neal Rainey gave her. Then he said, "You're very astute, Jody. And you're right. There was one in particular."

Jody decided to cover up her prying question. "But you finished your book and it's a big success. You must feel good about that."

"I do. But, mostly, it was good therapy. I ran a lot of . . . personal hang-ups out of my system."

Neal had hesitated, probably expecting Jody to make a comment about the book. She had to be honest with him. "I'm probably the only person in the United States who hasn't read it. Before today, I hadn't even heard about your book."

Neal laughed. "Really never heard about it?"

"Cross my heart. But I'd like to read it."

"Well, it just so happens that I have a copy in my suite," Neal said. "I don't know if assistant cruise directors have time for reading, but . . ."

"I'll always find time for reading," Jody said. "Although I don't usually read anything but . . ." She stopped herself short, embarrassed.

"Anything but what?" When Jody didn't reply, Neal said, "Let me guess. Beautiful, romantic stories about people in love." He was staring at her, the dark scrutiny felt more than seen in the uncertain light. "Am I right?"

Jody nodded. Was he making fun of her again? Defensively, she said, "I'm not going to apologize for that. I wish there was a lot more love in the world. So many terrible things happen. I want to read about . . . people caring about each other. Oh, having misunderstandings and quarrels, sure, but eventually I like to see love win out. You can call me a silly romantic fool, I don't care."

Neal turned, his hands reaching out to clasp Jody's shoulders. The move was so sudden that Jody caught her breath. She felt a shudder run through her body as Neal's fingers tightened against her flesh. Then she heard him murmur, "I don't think you're silly. And I don't think you're a fool. Jody, my profession deals with people who've done all sorts of hateful things to each other. I wish there was no need for people like me—middle-men who try to get some justice for the victims of all that hatred. If everyone in the world believed as strongly as you do in . . . in love, it would be a wonderful world."

She was touched, but Jody was also embarrassed. "It's . . . it's not that I don't think about anything else. . . ."

Neal was still holding her shoulders as he said, "I know that. The only people who think about love all the time are the ones who don't have enough of it in their lives. And I'm sure you do." There was a long pause, as if Neal was waiting for a reply. Then he said, "I presume that you do. That there's . . . somebody special."

His face was so close to hers, his questioning so strong and demanding that Jody felt compelled to give him another honest answer. "No. No, there's nobody special."

She heard him mutter something that sounded like

"Unbelievable?" Then in a swift motion that caught Jody unawares, he leaned down to place his lips against hers. It was a gentle kiss, chaste and brotherly, but it filled Jody with an alien surge of passion, an emotion she was sure he hadn't intended to stir inside her. When he lifted his lips from Jody's, taking his hands away from her shoulders, Neal said softly, "That was just because I find you sweet and honest and refreshing. I hope you understand?"

She hoped that the hammering of her heart was not audible. "Understand . . . what?"

"That I wasn't . . . that I'm not . . ." Neal released a quick laugh. "That kissing you was just an impulsive, friendly gesture."

Jody drew herself up to her full height. "I didn't think you had proposed marriage, Mr. Rainey. You're patronizing me again."

"No. No, I'm not." Neal sounded deadly serious. "I'm trying to be as honest as I find you. And I just want you to know that I'm not aboard looking for . . . any long-term involvements or . . . heavy commitments."

"Just your saying that is patronizing," Jody accused. "You make it sound as though you have to explain to me that I shouldn't get all starry-eyed just because . . . because some stranger made a . . . a friendly gesture after having behaved like an arrogant boor." She turned away from the rail. "I told you I liked to read romances. I didn't tell you I was dying to get involved in one!"

"I stand corrected again," Neal said. "And please don't go."

"It's late," Jody said. "I have to be up early. I'm not on vacation, remember?"

"And I have a speech to make," Neal said. Jody had started across the deck and he kept pace with her. His hand closed over Jody's elbow, guiding her, giving the lie to her words. Just the touch of his hand awoke the dormant desires inside her. His kiss may only have been a light, brotherly show of friendship to Neal, but Jody still felt the heat of his lips against her own, burning like fire. His closeness now was having a disquieting effect.

"Maybe we can see some of the islands together," Neal was saying. "It's no fun seeing interesting new places alone."

"Might be nice," Jody told him. She was sure it was the understatement of the century. Just the thought of seeing Puerto Rico with him tomorrow was a thrill beyond her wildest imaginings. But she had too much pride to admit that to a man who was so unpredictable. By morning he might forget that he had suggested that they see the islands together; she wasn't going to give him the satisfaction of demeaning her again.

At the elevator, Neal said suddenly, "Oh, do you have a minute? I promised you a copy of my book. That is, if you'd really like to read it."

"Of course I would." Jody let Neal lead her down a long corridor to where the ship's six most luxurious suites were located. She had a moment of uneasiness; alone and embittered, assuming that Jody was "available" because she had let him kiss her, he might be using his book as an excuse to lure her into his rooms. If he tries that, Jody told herself silently, I'll never speak to him again.

Was she relieved or slightly disappointed when Neal unlocked his door and entered without inviting her in? He was gone only a few seconds and then came back to the aisleway holding a hardcover book in his hand. "Don't feel obligated to read this," he said. "But if you do, you'll know me a little better." As he handed the book to Jody, he added, "I hope you'll want to know me better, Jody. As a friend."

Neal's photograph dominated the back of the book's

dust jacket. It was a portrait that didn't completely capture the sexy, masculine charisma of the man but came close enough. "Thank you," Jody said. "I'll get it back to you as soon as . . ."

"No, no, it's yours," Neal said.

Jody thanked him again. "And I'll want it autographed, if you don't mind. I've never met a real, live best-selling author before."

Neal's voice was husky and gentle. "I've never met a lovely assistant cruise director before."

They both laughed, and the laughter enhanced the warmth between them. For a moment Jody thought that he was going to reach out and kiss her again. Then, disappointingly, there was a sound that caught Neal's attention, the soft jangle of metal. Jody turned to see Diane Westbrook at the next door, fishing a key out of a small beaded evening bag. She looked somewhat bedraggled from her long night on the disco floor. Her long blond hair was disheveled and a weary expression clouded her beautiful face. As she started to fit the key into the lock, she turned to look directly at Neal. "Oh, hi, neighbor." Her voice was low and sultry, not in keeping with her youth.

Neal nodded and responded with a "Hi." Jody was ignored. She sensed that Diane wasn't too pleased to see Neal with her and no doubt didn't like getting caught returning to the suite she shared with her parents unescorted.

Neal added some inane, polite remark about "youngsters" who were able to enjoy dancing until dawn. For a few seconds Diane faced him with a look that spoke volumes. Her dark-lashed green eyes narrowed, sending the message that she was not a "youngster" but an intriguing woman who found Neal extremely attractive.

It was a brief exchange, but it left Jody less confident. She wanted to let him know, after seeing his bitterness and what seemed to be aloneness, that there were women who didn't lie and use and deceive. She had thought, for a few moments, that he was attracted to her. But she realized suddenly that the world was full of women who would love to console Neal Rainey; beautiful women from his own world of successful sophisticates.

Then, before she turned her key, Diane gave Jody a fleeting look of surprise, as though she wondered what exactly was the uninteresting, unglamorous aide to the cruise director doing outside Neal Rainey's suite at this hour of the morning. Diane's perfectly formed mouth curled up in a mysterious smile as she returned her gaze to Neal. "See you in the morning," she said pointedly.

Although there was no need for an escort, Neal insisted upon seeing Jody to her cabin on the Whitecap deck. They were at her door, Jody thanking him again for his book, when Neal raised one hand to place it on Jody's face. His fingers caressed her cheek, then ran tenderly over the outline of her lips. It was a gentle exploration, accompanied by the most poignant expression Jody had ever seen in a man's eyes. It seemed incredible that only hours ago this same man had reduced her to a seething rage.

Jody waited for something more. She was almost certain that he would clasp her in his arms, kiss her, perhaps ask to be invited into her cabin. She felt an urge to be closer to him, as though she were being drawn by a powerful magnet, and as Neal moved toward her, Jody drew in her breath. But he didn't kiss her again. His eyes were as dark as a clouded midnight, his voice so unsteady that it was hard to believe that this was a dynamic, aggressive attorney. He drew back abruptly, as if he might be afraid of being burned by a blazing fire. "While the trip lasts," he said, "let's see some of the Caribbean together."

There was nothing to do, after that, except to exchange good-nights. Then Neal was striding down the narrow hallway and Jody stepped into her cabin, her mind reeling.

How badly Neal must have been hurt to be this fearful about a closeness with another woman! He had kissed her, flattered her, told her that he wanted to see her again. But without telling Jody that he had loved and been seared by that love, he had let her know that she should expect nothing from him.

For a long time Jody lay sleepless on her bunk, trying to concentrate only on the thrill of being on a luxury liner, bound for exciting new places, actually being paid to enjoy this fabulous cruise. But her mind refused to shut out the events of the evening. Over and over again, she relived the warmth of Neal's kiss. She recalled his snide attitude toward her during their first two encounters, but her thoughts always returned to his compliment: "I've never met a lovely assistant cruise director before."

Was she being foolish, making something out of a casual incident and a few friendly words? Tomorrow Neal would probably be rushed by every single woman on board. And he had made it abundantly clear that he wanted no serious involvements.

Mingled with Jody's other thoughts about Neal and the excited pounding of her heart, was the recollection of Diane Westbrook's startling green eyes pouring out an undisguised jealousy and an even more formidable determination. Diane had made her interest in Neal very clear. And with all she had going for her, an attempt to compete with the beautiful blonde could only lead to misery.

Jody promised herself that she would be sensible. She would put Neal into perspective; he was just one of the many male passengers she would meet while working aboard the *Caribe Queen*. And he had said he didn't want to be any more than her friend. Until sleep finally overcame her, Jody tried to dismiss two thoughts that kept invading her consciousness: if Neal looked familiar to her, it was because she had met him and had him make love to her in thousands of daydreams. And she wanted to be more, much more, than his friend.

Chapter Three

In the morning, everything was blue and white and gold. A glorious sun brought out the intense blue of the sea and the sky was laced with delicate white clouds. The shores of Puerto Rico were in sight, entrancing the passengers who lined the rails and observation decks.

Jody spent a few moments with Prez MacCauley, who told her that he wanted her to familiarize herself with San Juan. "On future trips, I'll want you to relieve me of the burden of making my orientation speeches to the passengers," he said. "I'm going ashore with the artsy-craftsy teachers we have aboard. The attorneys are going with a professional tour guide. If Dr Allin is free, I'm sure he'd be happy to provide you with guide service."

Jody didn't tell Prez that she had been half-invited to go ashore with Neal Rainey. It had been a very indefinite date. What if he thought no more about it and she was left to visit the Puerto Rican city alone?

At the breakfast table, Jody noted that Diane Westbrook had been replaced by a bearded young graduate student whose consuming interest was his butterfly collection. The Westbrooks were eating in sullen silence and the three women from California were absorbed in a tour map of San Juan. Chatting with Dr. Allin, Jody stole a few surreptitious glances toward the table occupied by Neal Rainey and several of the other lawyers in his party. Not unexpectedly, Diane Westbrook was seated next to Neal. Seeing Neal's face lighted up with laughter, Jody felt a stab of jealousy. Seconds later, she wondered if it was wise to turn down the doctor's invitation on the slim hope that Neal might remember that he had asked her to see the islands with him.

"Prez said that he wants you to become an expert on our ports of call," Terry was saying. "I think I'm qualified to act as your tour guide. And I don't have any patients needing my services at the moment."

"It sounds wonderful," Jody told him. "But I have . . . tentative plans to go ashore with Mr. Rainey."

Terry's pale brows rose quizzically. "You've declared a truce? Last night you were telling me that he was an insufferable boor."

"He apologized," Jody said. "And you're right. The man has problems. He's been very badly hurt."

"The greatest ploy ever invented for attracting women," Terry said, spearing into a grilled sausage. "Brings out their maternal instincts. After that, they're hooked."

"Oh, he's just another passenger," Jody said. "And he wouldn't have been so rude to me if he had known who I am. It's not his fault that I wasn't wearing my ID pin."

Terry gave her a knowing look. "He's making a speech this morning," he said. "You won't get ashore until this afternoon."

Jody hadn't thought about that. But in spite of her uncertainty about the "date" with Neal, she said, "I'm sure you're more familiar with Puerto Rico than Mr. Rainey. And I *am* supposed to be learning from an expert. But a good way to get acquainted with a place is to get lost in it. Neal and I just might do that."

"I doubt it," the doctor said flatly. "He strikes me as a man who knows his way around." For an affable, uniformly pleasant man like Terry Allin, the words sounded strangely caustic and resentful.

During the rest of the meal, Jody heard something about the doctor's background. He had been a successful practitioner in an Atlanta suburb, married to a woman who couldn't cope with his long hours or with having her elegant dinner parties disrupted by emergency calls. They had had no children. Their divorce was "civilized" and Terry's wife was happily remarried. Two years ago, Terry had taken a vacation cruise aboard the *Caribe Queen*. The ship was in need of a new doctor and he had wanted a change. He had been aboard ever since.

"And you aren't tired of it yet?" Jody asked.

"I was beginning to get there," Terry said, smiling at Jody with a fondness that made her uncomfortable. "Then Prez had the good taste to hire a beautiful, intelligent new assistant. The ship has suddenly become interesting again. Hard to believe I met you only yesterday, Jody."

"It does seem that I've known you a lot longer," Jody said.

She had meant that the shipboard whirl had a way of distorting one's sense of time: days and nights could flow into each other, and if you didn't listen to the daily newscast, it was possible to forget that another, harsher world existed. Unfortunately, Terry Allin misinterpreted that casual comment. Jody felt the doctor's hand rest on hers for a moment. He sounded serious and encouraged as he said, "I'm glad you feel the same way I do, Jody. I'll miss being with you today, but we'll have many opportunities to get together. I look forward to it."

It would have been awkward to try to explain her simple statement. How could she tell Terry that she could never develop anything resembling a romantic interest in him? He was probably pursued by unmarried women during every cruise, but it was possible for people to be lonely in a crowd. Was he dissatisfied with his career, finding no satisfaction in curing hangovers and seasickness on a luxury cruiser? If his work wasn't meaningful to him and there was no really close relationship in his life, Terry was probably very vulnerable. Jody warned herself against being swept into another situation she couldn't handle. She was both relieved and elated as she saw Neal weaving his way between the tables toward her.

Neal looked radiantly handsome, his dark good looks accentuated by a white tropical leisure suit. There were few women whose eyes didn't follow his passage across the huge dining room. And what a thrill it was to hear him say, "I tried calling you, but you'd already left your cabin. You look beautiful, Jody. Are we still on for today?"

Jody returned his smile. "I wasn't sure. I thought you were going to be busy and . . ."

He looked concerned. "You didn't make another date?"

"No. No, I'm free."

"Beautiful! Everyone in my group is anxious to get ashore, so we've moved my speech forward so that I'll be finished by eleven. Meet you . . . where?"

They agreed to meet at the Rain Forest Bar on the topmost deck. Then, suddenly aware that there were other people present, Jody introduced Neal to the others at her table. After Neal had left the dining room, while the three women from California oh-ed and ah-ed, Jody heard the doctor say, "If he ever gets tired of practicing law, he can always go into the business of breaking hearts."

Terry's comment was not snide, but it contained just a trace of warning. He was probably right, Jody decided. How did she rate the attention of a man as dazzling as Neal Rainey? She would have to remember the doctor's remark and stop this ridiculous palpitation of the heart at the mere sight of Neal. And remember her less pleasant, original view of him. She would have to make certain that she didn't let him mean any more to her than she meant to him; someone to provide company while sightseeing.

Still, after she had learned the procedure of preparing the ship's daily schedule of activities, Jody left Prez's office and spent an inordinate amount of time getting dressed. And she was delighted when Neal met her at the appointed place exactly on time, his dark eyes noting the perfect waist-flattering fit of her floral print cotton. "You look lovely, Jody," he said. "I thought I'd never get out of that meeting, I was so anxious to be with you."

"How'd the speech go?" Jody asked. But his casual reply was lost in the excitement of having Neal link his arm through hers, his strong fingers intertwining with hers as he led her toward the elevator and the Nautilus deck, from which the movable stairway to the dock would lead them to shore.

A taxi took them through the narrow streets of Old San Juan to an enchanting plaza dominated by an ornate, towering church. It was all strange and exciting to Jody, but most thrilling of all was Neal's attention. She couldn't believe that this incredibly handsome, successful man was finding every excuse to hold her hand as they browsed through the quaint old shops and art galleries. Her hand was locked in Neal's, too, as they crossed a wide lawn that led them to the celebrated Morro Castle. Climbing steps or exploring the stone rooms of the celebrated fortress, reading signs that described its tumultuous history, Neal kept his fingers intertwined with Jody's, an occasional pressure conveying an intimacy that left her breath suspended in her lungs. He exuded an aura of maleness that affected her senses like heady wine.

Standing on a thick wall overlooking the cobalt sea as it dashed itself against the rocks far below, Neal slipped his arm around Jody's waist. Together they admired the enormous expanse of ultramarine and deep blue water. From their rocky promontory, it seemed that there was nothing in this world except beautiful sea and sky and the warmth of one body leaning closer against another. Did Neal sense this same powerful rapport? His nearness was almost frightening, sending small shivers through Jody's body, making her want to be even nearer to him.

After a long silence, Neal said softly, "This was going to be just a tourist sight for me. Being with you has made it an experience I'll never forget, Jody."

Their eyes met for a few seconds. It was as if Neal's dark eyes probed her very soul, Jody thought. She wanted to deny that she was overwhelmed by his touch, but Neal could read her secret thoughts. She was powerless to resist, even if she had wanted to, when he slipped both arms around her, pulling Jody against his steely hard body. One hand pressed against her back, imprinting the softness of her breasts against his firm chest. Then, lowering his head, Neal placed his lips against Jody's, gently at first, then more possessively, kissing her with a growing ardor that left her trembling and breathless when he finally released her mouth. In almost the same instant he took his arms away from her body, looking at her with a tender, smiling affection. "That was beautiful," he said. Jody noticed that he was breathing as hard as she was.

She could think of nothing to say. Her senses swimming, Jody felt that anything she said would sound hollow and trite. Finally, as they started the walk down the hill toward Old San Juan's meandering streets, Jody managed to say, "Do you . . . kiss all of your friends that way?"

Neal released a short laugh. "No. It just seemed right, somehow, with you."

"I'm reminding you," Jody said evenly, "that you were very emphatic last night about . . . not wanting any romantic involvements. We weren't going to be anything more than friends, remember?"

Neal threw an arm over Jody's shoulders casually.

"So we are. We're having a fun time and following an instinct to kiss you didn't do any harm." He sounded light and carefree, as though his kiss was not still burning on Jody's lips. Was he only pretending indifference, or had that prolonged meeting of their lips left him completely unmoved?

Jody felt let down. Some of the anger she had experienced in her first meetings with Neal returned. Then she remembered that she *had* been warned, not only by Terry Allin, but by Neal himself. If she was fool enough to make something out of an impulsive kiss, it was her own fault. She made up her mind not to let herself be swayed again.

Yet, later that day, while they strolled one of Puerto Rico's glistening white beaches, it happened again, so easily and so instinctively, that Jody could hardly believe that she was being held in a fierce, wanting embrace, and that her own lips and body were responding to Neal's growing fervor with an intensity that matched his. As he held her pinned against him, Jody's reaction was mindless; her arms crept around Neal's neck, then her fingers strayed to the back of his head, pressing his face hard against her own as he showered her cheeks, her temple, then her mouth once more, with kisses that were like searing brands against her flesh.

Neal released her as abruptly as he had before, infuriating Jody with the impression that she was his to reach out for when the mood struck him and to be cast aside when he had satisfied his momentary whim. Why had she let him know with her response that she was his to be toyed with whenever he chose to pull her into his arms? She barely knew this man; how could she have returned his kisses with a fire that she had never known before, never knew she was capable of?

Then, contrastingly, he was walking beside her as though they were just a pair of tourists who had been thrown together for a day of sightseeing. His switch from one mood to another was puzzling. Had he simply given in to a fleeting physical urge that could be forgotten in the next second? Or, having been deeply hurt, was he afraid to become a slave to his emotions, blithely waving away a brief show of passion as though it would go away if it were ignored? Jody found it hard to get her breath. Walking beside Neal as they visited charming Old World boutiques and admired colorful folk art, she was torn between annoyance with herself for having let Neal manipulate her so easily and with wondering if he would take her into his arms again before their time together had ended.

Jody tried to concentrate on the experience of being in a strange and fascinating place. Local residents chattered in Spanish as they brushed by Jody and Neal on the narrow sidewalks. Tourists laden with hand-crafted gift items smiled as they passed, all of them enthralled by the myriad sights and sounds of this beautiful island, so American in its industriousness and still clinging proudly to its unique culture. Their tour of the old walled section of San Juan would have been fascinating in any case; seeing this restored area of balconied buildings under a brilliant blue sky, painted with fluffy white clouds, in the company of a man who seemed to turn every female head as he walked by, was a sensation beyond Jody's most thrilling day-dreams.

Neal was chatting amiably and impersonally as they visited the Pablo Casals Museum, where the famed cellist's works were preserved on tape. He marveled at the contrasts in architecture when they taxied to the strand of ultra-modern hotels and shops that lined the fabulous Condado, the city's luxury strip along the beach. Jody only half-heard Neal's comments; she was still in a daze from the stirring contact with him. Determined not to let him know his effect upon her, Jody pretended the same easy-going casualness that Neal had assumed. And she was able to laugh when he said, "I'm sure you would have seen more of the highlights if you'd had an experienced guide. But if we hadn't gotten lost, we wouldn't have found this place."

Neal was referring to a tiny restaurant, well away from the glitter of the Condado; intriguing aromas poured from an open doorway.

"Funny," Jody said. "I told Dr. Allin that the best way to get acquainted with a city is to get lost in it."

As they found a table in the dimly lighted little restaurant, Neal shot Jody a dark glance. "Did he offer to squire you around today?"

"He . . . would have, but he's too busy," Jody said. "And, as he said, there'll be plenty of opportunities later. This isn't an only trip for me. And he's been aboard the ship for . . . I think two years."

Neal was quiet for a time, scowling at a menu that was placed before him by a young waiter. Then, sounding positively surly, he said, "Well, I won't be around for the next cruise. You'll be able to make up for lost time." It was absurd, but Neal spoke in a resentful tone. He couldn't possibly be jealous; he must know that Jody and the doctor had just met the day before. Besides, Neal had been so emphatic about letting Jody know that he would never be more than her friend. No, probably not even a friend; when this vacation trip was over, he would go back to San Francisco and remember Jody the way one remembers ships that pass in the night. But maybe, having been humiliated by another man, he felt competitive with all men, even when there was no reason for it.

Their mood turned jovial again as they discovered the savory appeal of Puerto Rico's national dish, *arroz con pollo*, and as Jody was introduced to *coquito*, a sweet drink that made her think of coconut syrup.

"Too sweet for my taste," Neal said as he took a sip from Jody's glass. "Glad I ordered Puerto Rican beer." His eyes lingered on Jody's face, shining with admiration that brought a rush of warmth to her temples. "I like my food and drink pungent. And my company beautiful and sweet."

As Neal's eyes dropped to the visible cleft between her breasts, she felt a tremulousness that threatened to betray her confused emotions. She could barely look at Neal without trembling, yet the sight of him was irresistible. Strong and virile, amazingly muscular for a man who followed a profession that placed few physical demands upon him, Neal seemed to glow with undeniable masculinity. Jody's concentration dropped to a safer view as she studied his hands, the long, sensitive fingers, the strength of his wrists, the dark hairs that added to his overt maleness. Did he know that his physical appearance alone evoked a blistering desire in her? He *had* to know. He probably knew exactly what Jody was feeling.

Jody was both disappointed and relieved when Neal took on a brotherly attitude as they lingered over their late lunch. She felt rejected one moment and then, in the next, was glad that Neal wasn't tempting her with looks and touches that she might not be able to resist.

It was easier on her emotions when they left the restaurant and resumed their exploration of the maze of streets, returning by taxi to Old Town because it had more appeal than the Miami-like newer section of town. They were like children, then, happy to be together, delighted with every new and unfamiliar sight. Neal regretted that there wouldn't be time to drive out to El Yunque, the spectacular rain forest on the other side of the island. But the *Caribe Queen* would return to Puerto Rico after its circle of the Caribbean. "I'd like to see the jungle with you," Neal said matter-of-factly. "And what's the name of that mountain I read about? Supposed to be blindingly green . . . hundreds of waterfalls. . . ."

"El Verde," Jody remembered from a guidebook. "Maybe we can see it when we come back here. Oh, I want to see everything, Neal! The little villages with the palm-thatched rooftops and more of the beaches and . . . I can do without the casinos and the discos, but wouldn't you love to see a big festival? I hear they have them at the drop of a hat."

"You're like a little girl," Neal said fondly. "I love your enthusiasm. I get annoyed, thinking back to dates with . . ." He stopped, it seemed, just short of mentioning a name. Then he went on, ". . . dates with women who think it's unsophisticated to get a childish kick out of something as simple as a little village fair. They can't let go of that blasé facade."

Was he talking about the woman he had loved and who had cheated on him? Terry had said that Neal's fiancée had been a "socialite." If he had married her, in time would Neal have become disenchanted with the aloof attitude he was describing now? Or was this a sour-grapes reaction; since he had lost his love, was he looking for justifications? Jody didn't know the answer and she couldn't ask.

They had changed the subject to a less personal line of conversation as sunset darkened the softly lighted streets of Old San Juan. And Neal was again a light-hearted companion as he steered Jody down the stone stairway that led to a cellar cabaret.

"You seem to know where you're going," Jody commented.

"I do. The ship's bulletin said this is one place we shouldn't miss. Supposed to have the best flamenco artists this side of Barcelona." As they descended into a dark, cavernous and crowded room, Neal added, "This place is called *El Gato Blanco*. The White Cat, if you've forgotten your high school Spanish."

A resplendently clad waiter greeted them and apologized; there were no private tables available. Would they mind sitting with a small party from one of the visiting cruise ships?

Seconds later, Jody found herself seated at a table

that included not only Dr. Terry Allin, but a ravishing blond beauty who looked from Jody to Neal and then back to Jody again with an expression in her green eyes that, even in the semi-darkness of the White Cat Club, made Diane Westbrook look, for a moment, like the most malevolent person Jody had ever seen.

Chapter Four

There was no one on the postage stamp-sized dance floor or on the stage at the moment. Diane's father, who was also seated at the crowded table, was making up for the lack of entertainment by being a little too loud and gauche, earning annoyed glances from his beautiful young daughter. Mrs. Westbrook was nowhere in sight, and when Jody asked about her, Dalton Westbrook said, "She wasn't up to it."

There was an awkward tension around the table. The doctor was playing the part of the expert traveler, which Neal seemed to resent.

"There's time to order dinner before the first show begins," Terry advised. "Have the *paella Valenciana*," he advised Jody.

"We had a rice dish for lunch," Neal said curtly.

Terry shrugged, remaining cheerful in spite of the chilly rebuff. "But the Spaniards handle it with more flamboyance," he persisted. "They throw in everything but the kitchen blender. Shellfish, poultry—if it swims or flies, you'll find it in the spectacular *paella* they serve here. It's an experience Jody shouldn't miss."

"I usually let my dates make their own selection from the menu," Neal countered. He seemed pleased when Jody followed his lead and ordered a steak. The doctor shrugged again, telling Jody that there was "always the next time we're here in port."

How childish men could be, Jody thought. Neal had assumed a proprietary air, his arm over the back of her

59

chair while Terry addressed most of his comments to her. It seemed incredible to be getting this much male attention when just across the table was a ravishingly attractive young woman who was making every effort to impress Neal.

Jody was relieved when the floor show began; the conversation at the table was getting too strained for comfort. She wished that she could have spent this evening alone with Neal, but since that hadn't happened, it was good to have the distraction of flashily dressed flamenco dancers clicking their heels on the wooden-floored stage, to applaud a young male guitarist's version of "Malaguena" and then to hear another, older man defy the range of the human voice in a tearful Spanish ballad.

When the cheers and wild applause died down, Terry said, "Isn't it sad to think that the man's life is going to be considerably shortened in exchange for this hand-clapping approval?" He paused, apparently waiting for someone to ask him to explain his statement.

Neal didn't give the doctor that opportunity. Casually, as though having a head full of obscure knowledge should be expected of him, he said, "Yes, all *falsetto* singers destroy themselves young."

Why had Neal found it necessary to deny the doctor his chance to display his specialized knowledge? Jody pondered the thought all through the next Spanish bolero, concluding that Neal's professional confidence in himself was not at stake. It was his personal loss that had shaken him. And he seemed to glow with interest when Diane smiled at him admiringly and said, "You know so many things, Mr. Rainey! I suppose you have to, defending so many different kinds of people. I know when I was reading your book, I was amazed at what you had to learn about . . . everything from poodle breeding to building solar reflectors."

"I just did spot research," Neal said in a pleasant tone. He appeared pleased, and Jody thought, "Score one for Miss Westbrook." She felt foolish, not having read Neal's best-seller when even this seemingly shallow girl was familiar with it.

Dalton Westbrook reminded his daughter that "book education" wasn't all that necessary to success. His lucrative contracting business was proof of that, wasn't it? He'd only gone through the eighth grade, but, by golly, he was able to send Diane to the best schools in the United States and Europe, right?

Diane and Neal exchanged indulgent, secretive little smiles and Jody found herself feeling excluded. Men! Did they always have to be aggressive, defending their delicate egos? She turned to Terry and deliberately gave him a chance to shine, asking him about points of interest in San Juan that she might have missed thus far. It was during this disjointed cross-conversation that she looked up to see Prez MacCauley at the foot of the stone entry stairway. Seeing him across the room, Jody thought he looked like a wraith, appearing suddenly in the smoke-filled cabaret, looking around with wide, searching eyes. Then she saw Prez snaking his way around the crowded tables until he stopped between two that were occupied exclusively by *Caribe Queen* passengers. He looked pale and somewhat distraught. Barely nodding at the others, he leaned down toward Terry Allin. "Knew I'd find you here, Doc. Emergency."

Terry was on his feet in an instant. "What is it?"

Prez spoke in a hushed whisper. Only Terry and Jody were close enough to hear him. "Mrs. Westbrook. I'll tell her husband and daughter. Get back to the ship as fast as you can and I'll follow you with the family." Even more quietly, Prez added, "It might be her appendix."

Terry excused himself and hurried toward the stairway. And then Prez, the soul of discretion, said, "Mr. Westbrook, could I talk to you privately for a moment?"

Shortly afterward, Diane Westbrook and her father, with Prez in the lead, ascended the stairway to the street.

"What was that all about?" Neal wanted to know.

Jody remembered that she was a member of the ship's staff. "A . . . medical problem. Nothing serious, I'm sure."

"Mrs. Westbrook?" Neal guessed. When Jody held her silence, he smiled faintly and said, "I wouldn't want you as an unfriendly witness, Jody. You know when not to talk."

Jody accepted his remark as a compliment. Maybe she should have offered to go back to the ship with the others, but she decided that Prez would prefer that she stay here to keep the other passengers from knowing that anything was wrong. She breathed a silent prayer for the unhappy woman who was Diane's mother, sipped from the *pina colada* Neal had ordered for her, and ignored his statement: "Their suite is right next to mine, you know. They're constantly bickering out in the hall. I really do feel sorry for that lovely little girl of theirs."

Was he so naive that he didn't realize that their daughter was probably the cause of the Westbrooks' arguments? One didn't gossip about the passengers; that was another rule Jody decided to observe. She tried to mask her sudden jealousy, agreeing that Diane was, indeed, lovely, but hardly a "little girl."

"Yes, she's quite grown up," Neal admitted. "And old enough to have developed quite an impressive backhand. She was on the tennis court while I was waiting for you this morning after my speech. I'll have to ask her for a game before this trip's over."

It was getting more difficult to pretend indifference. "Yes, we like our passengers to take advantage of all the recreational facilities."

She had sounded so prim, so artificial, that Neal had apparently seen through her jealousy. In any case, he started to laugh, which only served to infuriate Jody. And then, conversely, Neal was sounding like a petty, possessive lover instead of just a friendly escort-for-the-day. "I'm sorry the doctor was called away. You seemed to be enjoying your little tête-a-tête with him."

Jody made a whooping sound. "My *what?*"

"You can't deny that you were enjoying his attention. You practically ignored me for a while there."

Jody could only stare at Neal in disbelief.

"And this morning, at breakfast, when I walked over to your table, you were holding hands."

"We were doing nothing of the sort!" Jody corrected. "He . . . he was giving me some advice and . . . I think he patted my hand. He's a nice, fatherly . . ."

Neal rolled his eyes ceilingward. "Fatherly. Oh, sure!"

Was this jealousy? If so, it struck Jody as absurd. Yet she couldn't help saying, "Terry's going to be a big help to me. I've admitted to him my apprehensions about this job. I mean, I don't know what people are supposed to wear, or what they should see on the islands. He's been on the ship long enough to be able to give me all sorts of advice." Why did she feel she had to explain? Jody thought suddenly. "I happen to like the doctor. He's nice people. And if he likes me, there's no harm in that."

"I can't help thinking that he does," Neal said in an edgy tone. "And he's great at giving advice. Even to telling my date what she should have for dinner."

"That's ridiculous," Jody countered. "He was just trying to be helpful."

"I've always managed to see that any woman I was out with enjoyed herself without any outside help. But, then, I didn't know that the two of you were that close."

"*Close?*" Jody shrilled the word. "I haven't known him as long as I've known you."

"But you managed to get fairly close to me in that

short length of time." Neal's proprietary air made no sense to Jody at all. Nor did his cutting remark: "You didn't exactly fight me off at Morro Castle."

Jody drew a quick breath. "Of all the . . ." She stopped, flooded with a resurgence of the same fury that Neal had brought out in her during their first two meetings. Yesterday? Was that really only yesterday? This afternoon she had been feeling as though she had known Neal all of her life. She had felt warm and close and excited by him. Now he was sounding like the boor who had humiliated her on the ship when she had only been trying to do her job. She wanted to get up and walk away from the table. How could Neal have cheapened those moments together with a statement like that?

And he wasn't finished, apparently. "Well, I don't suppose it's that unusual for fellow crew members to get acquainted in a hurry. Or for you to get friendly with passengers as fast as possible." Neal didn't sound like the same man who had made Jody feel so happy, so relaxed, so ecstatic all day. He sounded surly and possessive, as though a few kisses had given him that right. "Isn't that the name of the game on cruise ships? Cram in as much as you can while the cramming's good?"

"If you're talking about sightseeing, I agree with you," Jody said, her voice rising. What right did Neal have to goad her this way, making implications that he had to know were insulting? "But you're not talking about sightseeing, are you? You're making me sound cheap and available because the ship's doctor patted my hand at the breakfast table. Surrounded by other people, in broad daylight, and . . ."

"I'll admit it was hardly a passionate tryst," Neal conceded. "But surely you're not so naive that you don't know the man's enchanted with you. Something you hardly discouraged tonight."

Jody couldn't believe what she was hearing. The

sudden change in him had her so incensed that she was shaking. "I don't know what you're getting at, Mr. Rainey. But even if everything you're saying was true, it wouldn't be any of your business."

"Maybe it wouldn't be if you hadn't been quite so . . . encouraging with me." Neal's eyes, black as ebony, shone with a derisive glint. "And you won't deny that you were coming on very strong with me."

"I've . . ." Jody stopped to catch her breath. "I've never met anyone as smug as you!" She wanted to cry out that she had not been "encouraging" Neal, that she had not been "coming on strong." But the moments during which Neal had held her in his arms were too fresh in her mind. His kisses were too indelibly printed on her lips. And, even now, the searing, steely hardness of his body pressed against hers was not just remembered but felt. How could she deny that she had responded to Neal's heated embraces with a fire that matched his? She felt confused and embarrassed. How could he be cruel enough to criticize her and then remind her that she had behaved like an easy conquest? She felt tears welling in her eyes. More quietly now, because she was aware of other people seated nearby listening, Jody said, "I'm not very experienced with men. Especially not slick, sophisticated lawyers who like to brag about . . . women not being able to resist them." Her tears had spilled over and Jody swiped at them with the back of her hand. "I only let you kiss me because I . . . because you . . ."

Neal's eyes challenged her. "Yes?"

She had no words to explain why she had melted in his arms, returning the fire of his kisses. How could she tell him that for a few brief moments she had been swept by a floodtide of emotions? Tell him that she had been powerless to resist the strongest physical attraction she had ever experienced? Tell him she had believed, while he held her in his arms, that he was as sincere as she was? Fool! Now, just because another man had spoken to her, his rapacious ego demanded that he hurl insults at her.

Music had started up again. Jody forced her voice to sound calm. Over the sound of flamenco guitars she said, "You were the one who said you didn't want a serious involvement with any woman. Well, I happen to feel the same way. And a few kisses don't give you the right to act as though you . . . you own me." Tossing her head with a show of defiance she did not feel inside, Jody added, "I'm in my twenties. There's a whole big world out there, so don't get the idea that I'm even remotely interested in being tied down . . . to you or anybody else."

"I didn't think we had discussed marriage," Neal said caustically.

Jody realized that she was no match for him. "I don't think I'd even want you for a friend. You don't know how to be one!"

"Fine. We understand each other." Neal's expression was one of cold contempt. "It's a pity, though. I could have used a friend to help keep the husband-hunters at bay so that I could enjoy my vacation."

Jody gasped. It no longer mattered if anyone else was hearing what she had to tell this insufferable person. "You're actually admitting that you were going to *use* me? You actually are conceited enough to think every woman on board that ship is going to fall insanely in love with you?" She tried to fake a ridiculing laugh, but her tears gave her away. Jody groped for her handbag which was wedged between two chairs. "You're a hateful excuse for a human being!"

"I thought assistant cruise directors were supposed to help the passengers enjoy the trip." Neal turned away from Jody, staring toward the performers on stage as if she were beneath his notice. "Or are you practicing first with the ship's personnel?"

Jody glared at him, seething inside. "I'll see to it that you don't miss any cocktail parties, Mr. Rainey. I'll reserve a tennis court for when you want it. But I wasn't hired to protect you from all the women on board who have the bad taste to think you're Mr. Wonderful." She got to her feet as the musical number was concluded. Before Neal could react, she had left the table, threading her way through the narrow aisles toward the stairway. She was determined not to cry, holding her head up and trying to present a picture of composure to anyone who watched her hurried exit. She was near the foot of the stairway when she heard Neal call, "Jody, wait! Let me take care of the check and see you to the ship!"

Jody ignored him. She would find her own taxi. Sick at heart, she made her way up the stone steps, then found herself standing in front of the cabaret, alone, feeling lost, suddenly frightened. She was in a strange city on a dimly lighted narrow street. There was no cab in sight.

Two men approached, sending Jody into a panic. Should she run back down the stairs? Before she could move, the men had passed, one of them looking her over questioningly, the other making an inviting, eyebrow-lifting grimace. Both turned back to look at Jody, then kept sauntering down the street. She could feel her heart pounding. Should she face the embarrassment of going back to the club and asking someone to phone for a cab? She had run off blindly and now . . .

Now a hand closed over Jody's elbow and she shrieked in terror. Then she heard Neal's voice saying, "Crazy female! You ought to know better than to be out here alone!"

Jody released her breath, then jerked away from Neal's touch. "I was fine until you sneaked up behind me and . . . startled me."

"I didn't sneak up behind you," Neal shouted. "I came up the stairs and there you were. Jody, this is ridiculous. We shouldn't be fighting with each other. I don't know what got into me. I seem to have a talent for making you miserable."

Pride demanded that Jody tell Neal to leave her alone, but she didn't want him to go. She felt safe and secure again with Neal standing beside her. Yet she was furious with herself for being grateful that he had not let her go back to the ship alone. As angry as she was with him, somehow she was happy to have him caring for her, looking after her again. It made no sense, no sense at all!

As though Neal's powerful personality could produce miracles, a cab materialized and skidded to the curb. Jody let Neal help her into the back seat. Then, as he settled beside her, giving instructions to the driver in enviably clear Spanish, Jody felt a reassuring pat on her hand. He was telling her that he knew she had been frightened at the thought of being alone.

A short ride to the docks and then they were walking up the stepped gangplank of the *Caribe Queen.* "It was such a great day," Neal was saying. "Why did it have to be spoiled at the end?"

"Because you made a big issue out of my having a conversation with a man I'm going to be working with," Jody said pointedly. "And since you're the one who made it very clear that we're *only* going to be friends, I didn't think that meant I wasn't allowed to have other friends, too."

Jody glanced at Neal for his reaction. He looked somewhat sheepish and he nodded. "You're right. And I'm sorry. I'm truly sorry, Jody."

They were on the Nautilus deck, close to the glass doors through which they must pass to get to the nearest elevator. Would they part on this melancholy note? Would they avoid each other for the rest of the cruise? Jody's heart felt heavy. As changeable as Neal was, he brought out a disturbing ambivalence in her, too. She didn't want the evening to end. And she hesitated only a moment when Neal said, "It's getting close to sailing time, isn't it?"

"It can't be. All those people at the club would miss the boat."

Neal peered at his watch. "You're right. It's still another hour and a half before we sail. Beautiful out. Couldn't we stay on the deck and . . . talk awhile?"

"Well, I . . . have to be up early in the morning," Jody told him. She paused a split second. "But it would be exciting to see the ship pulling away from the dock at midnight."

She saw a gentle smile on Neal's face. Then he was guiding her to the aft rail. There were few people on the deck. Those who were not still ashore were probably in the casino or listening to the calypso band in one of the lounges. Neal took Jody's arm, holding it with a tenderness that suggested she might break, yet firmly, as though he was afraid she might disappear. The air could not have been balmier, the starlight more awesome, the twinkling lights of the city more dramatic. They propped their arms on the high railing and looked toward the brilliance that is San Juan at night. Neal repeated what he had said earlier: "I'm sorry about tonight, Jody. I don't know what made me act the way I did. Like a jealous, possessive lover instead of . . . a traveling buddy."

Jody sensed that he wanted to do the talking, that he had more to say to her. She was silent, waiting for Neal to go on.

"It's hard to explain, even for someone as verbal as I am. I seem to find exactly the right words when I'm addressing a jury, but right now . . . I'm at a loss. Without going into a long personal history that would probably bore you, I can't tell you why I felt suddenly resentful tonight. As though someone was . . . trying to take something—someone—away from me. Foolish, of course. You never said that you did. But I liked it better when we were alone together. I didn't like someone else taking up any of your time or attention."

"I should think you'd feel more secure," Jody commented. "You have everything possible going for you. Even if I was more than just a . . . a new acquaintance, really, why would you presume that I found someone else more interesting than you?"

"It's happened," Neal said in a barely audible voice. Then, dismissing that thought without going into an explanation, he said, "I know what you're suggesting, I'm supposed to have the world at my doorstep. And in terms of quantity, I probably do. That doesn't mean that I'm not . . ."

Jody waited for him to finish his sentence, but Neal was staring toward the panorama of lights. "That doesn't mean that you don't ever feel lonely?" she ventured.

Neal let out a short dismissing laugh. "Lonely? Ohh . . . I manage to stay occupied," he said. But there was an untypical lack of confidence in his tone. Had she touched a sore spot in this man who was usually so self-assured that he often sounded arrogant?

Jody persisted. "You get lots of invitations, women pursue you, probably get a ton of fan mail now that you're a successful author." She pondered the point she was getting at for a moment. "That doesn't serve the same purpose as feeling that you're . . . that you're really communicating with one other human being, does it?" And where had *that* come from? Jody wondered. She was coming on like a sage old philosopher instead of the inexperienced, naive young woman Neal knew her to be. She hoped he wouldn't laugh at her.

Neal didn't. He took his arms from the rail, reached out for Jody's shoulders, pulling her from the rail and turning her around so that he could look at her. She felt the warmth of his fingers against her bare skin, an electric thrill darting through her at the intimate contact. Incredible that less than half an hour ago she had found him despicable!

Neal's voice was a husky low whisper. His eyes fixed Jody's with a hypnotic gaze from which she could not turn away. "You're wasted as an assistant cruise director, Jody. You'd make a great psychologist."

Meeting Neal's intense gaze was an overwhelming sensation. Jody's voice trembled, just as her body had started to tremble. "I . . . didn't mean to sound as though I . . . know all about life. Or anything about you, Neal. I was just trying to understand why someone like you could . . ."

"Could be jealous and petty? Yes, and lonely. Needing to communicate on a one-to-one basis with another human being." Neal's arms closed around Jody easily and naturally. And just as easily and naturally she let herself be held. There was one moment when she felt that he was a stranger, an unpredictable stranger who had made her feel cheap because she had let him kiss her earlier today. But the disturbing thought was erased from Jody's mind as Neal's lips closed over hers in a kiss that was so gentle that it brought an ache to her throat. He could make her want to laugh and to cry in the same instant. Then, as the kiss lingered, the pressure increasing, the caress of Neal's hands running over Jody's body more and more demanding, she felt as though she would never again draw a full breath. The intensity of his maleness became known as Neal pressed her closer against him and his mouth rained more heated kisses over her face. When he lifted his lips from hers, his voice was like a sighing wind: "Jody, Jody, Jody," he repeated. It was the joyous sound of discovery, but it was a pained cry for love and understanding, too. "Jody . . . you're so beautiful, so right in my arms!"

She had not put her arms around him, holding back because he had reminded her tonight that her responses had been filled with an ardor that matched his. Now Neal dropped her from his embrace, taking Jody's wrists in his hands and placing them around his neck. "Hold me, too, Jody," he whispered. His voice was deep and tense with emotion. "Hold me, darling. Tonight I need to be held."

She would not have believed a man could be so powerful and so tender at the same time. Neal was a study in contrasts, a puzzling, enigmatic, almost frightening intense man. Yet, though her entire being felt as though it was on fire, though her yearning for him had engulfed her mind and her body, she felt that she *belonged* in Neal's arms. There was no one around to observe them, as there had been this afternoon. Was that why Neal dared more intimate caresses? Was that why his hand found Jody's breast, exploring the softness as his eyes possessed hers? It was almost more than she could bear, Jody thought. She was gasping for breath after another prolonged kiss, pressed so hard against him now that she wondered what possession must be like; could any two people be fused more closely together? Yes. Yes, they could. The thought intoxicated her senses. All her resistance was swept away in a floodtide of passion as Neal's tongue explored her mouth. Swaying, locked together, it seemed that what they were sharing now was more important than breathing.

When Neal finally let her go, his powerful chest rising and falling with breathlessness, he murmured, "We'd better stop. In another minute I'm going to be inviting you to my suite."

She was determined to say no, but just the suggestion was exciting to Jody. She had to stop Neal now; more important, she had to place a rein on her own emotions. He was too magnetic and she was too vulnerable. And she had to keep reminding herself that she didn't really know this man. She was toying with a searing flame, coming too close for safety. For wasn't this what happened to your mind and to your body when you started to fall in love? And wasn't falling in love with this dynamic, exasperating, overpowering puzzle of a man anything but a one-way road to Heartbreak City?

"You don't invite 'just friends' to your room," Jody managed to say. She also managed a sly smile that she hoped would remind him that he had set the rules for this insane game they were playing and that she intended to abide by them. Yes, they were physically attracted to each other. Yes, she had responded to his kisses, had let him caress her more intimately than any man had caressed her before. But she wasn't going to let him think that he had brought her to a fever pitch that had burned out her power to reason. Reasoning, she knew that going to Neal's suite would be a mistake. Tomorrow, in one of his less pleasant moods, he would not be able to remind her that she was an easy conquest.

A long time later, after they had watched another cruise ship depart from the harbor, glittering with lights, its decks crowded with excited passengers, they lingered until the *Caribe Queen* eased away from the harbor and out to sea. They were silent, holding hands as they watched the beautifully lighted shoreline fade. And when, at last, Jody said that it was time for her to get some sleep, Neal's good-night kiss at her cabin door was no more than a brotherly peck on her temple. "Tomorrow," he said softly. "Curaçao. Let's see it together if we can."

"If we can," Jody repeated. Then he was striding down the hallway, back to the elevator.

Jody fell across her bed, her heart still racing. She knew sleep would be a long time coming, in spite of the long, active day filled with surprises. She tried to think of other things; how was Elise Westbrook doing? Prez had not indicated that Elise's condition was serious. Terry would know what to do.

There was no point in even trying to think about

anyone else. There was only one face before her, only one voice repeating, "Jody, Jody, Jody!" Neal was a thrill and a threat and a confusion; Jody's arms ached for him. She imagined him here in her small cabin, holding her, touching her, kissing her, making love to her. Although the cabin was comfortably air-conditioned, her body felt as though she were lying down on the steamy floor of a jungle. And the most handsome man in the world was gazing at her with passionate desire, his hands adding to the heat of her body and her senses, his deep, husky voice saying over and over and over again, "Jody . . . Jody . . . Jody!"

Chapter Five

Jody slept through breakfast. She was disappointed; in the dining room she would have seen Neal. He had said something about their seeing Curaçao together; would he remember that this morning? Would he contact her before the *Caribe Queen* sailed into the quaint Dutch port?

Reporting for duty, she found Prez MacCauley in his office conferring with some of the attorneys. They were there, Jody learned, to plan a private cocktail party for their group. "Make sure the day's program gets delivered to all the passengers," Prez said. He waved one hand, dismissing her, making Jody feel superfluous.

The head steward all but glared at Jody when she asked Prez's question about the day's activity sheets. He had been supervising the distribution of the programs for more than a year and resented being questioned, especially by a new member of the staff.

Jody made a tour of the top deck. No one in need of recreational supervision there. An exercise class was in progress. A few people were playing water volleyball in the pool, and billiard and Ping-Pong tables were in use. Although she greeted a number of people, Jody felt unnecessary. She noticed Dalton Westbrook sitting at the Rain Forest Bar, drink in hand even at this early hour. She considered asking about his wife, who hadn't had appendicitis after all, but decided to avoid the subject . . . and to avoid him.

For a few minutes Jody stood at the rail, looking out

at the sea. It was a gigantic sapphire this morning, its intense blues and greens sparkling under a cloudless sky like a huge, million-karat gem. How thrilling it was to be aboard this luxury liner, how exciting it would be to see an exotic island like Curaçao! And, yesterday, San Juan had been . . .

San Juan had been the place where Neal Rainey had taken her into his arms and kissed her. Jody felt guilty enough about not doing much to earn her salary. She should at least be thinking about her new job. But it seemed that her mind crowded out every thought that did not concern Neal. Would he be busy with his attorney friends today—too busy to remember what he had said about seeing Curaçao with her? If he was going to contact her, would he telephone the cruise director's office?

Jody was walking toward the outside stairway to the deck below when she saw him. Neal, racing across the tennis court, slamming a ball across the net with a sure, powerful stroke, looking like a bronzed Greek god in a white T-shirt and tennis shorts. His movements were like those of a graceful jungle cat. Admiring the straining leg muscles, looking at a body that was pure male perfection, Jody found herself mixing metaphors as she compared him with every living creature that is physically ideal. His dark hair flashed pinpoints of light under the golden morning sun. Jody stood entranced, staring in admiration, seeing only the man who had held her in his arms last night, touched her breasts, whispered her name in an adoring tone. It was some time before Jody's eyes followed the tennis ball over the net and saw another figure of perfection. Equally tanned, equally graceful, equally energetic, and, obviously an expert player who was giving Neal a stimulating challenge. Diane Westbrook was like a carefully matched female complement. Her long blond hair whipped by the soft breeze, her smile as white and dazzling as the sleekly fitted tennis dress that hugged her lithe young figure, she was a sight that couldn't help but set a man's heart racing.

It was silly to feel left out, like some wallflower left on the sidelines. Tennis was Neal's passion, he had told her. He had found an accomplished partner. How utterly stupid it was to feel this gnawing envy inside. I'm supposed to be here working, Jody reminded herself. These are two passengers, people on vacation, the people who make my salary possible. But rationalizing didn't ease the heaviness she felt. It didn't even help to remember that she had thought Neal presumptuous last night when he had resented her attention from Terry Allin. He had admitted that jealousy on his part had been out of line. I'm being an idiot, Jody lectured herself silently. Time to find something useful to do.

She had started to turn away when Neal slammed a ball over the net, catching Diane off guard on the wrong side of the court. She ran for it, racquet poised for a return, but she was far too late. The ball hit the back enclosure. She made a pretense of throwing her racquet to the ground in disgust with herself, but then laughed, tossing her beautiful golden mane as she ran toward the net. Neal, smiling broadly, pleased with himself, had run to meet her. There was a sportsmanlike handshake and then, as Jody's spirits plummeted, a warm, impetuous hug over the net. They looked extremely happy, Neal delighted with his triumph, Diane playing up to his male ego with what must surely be a practiced technique. Perhaps, Jody thought with an unwarranted bitterness, perhaps she could have beat him at his own game.

Jody was still standing outside the fence when Neal circled the court. He and Diane were laughing, chatting excitedly as they walked out of the enclosed area. Jody saw Diane link her arm through Neal's. He took her hand, giving it a visible squeeze. Mr. and Miss Perfection, Jody thought. There was no logic to the tears that had blurred her vision. She hurried toward the steel steps, hoping that neither Diane nor Neal had seen her watching.

Jody returned to Prez's office to find that the meeting with Neal's colleagues was over and Prez was in the observation lounge giving an orientation talk to passengers who would be going ashore in a few hours. Sitting at the small desk that had been assigned to her, Jody noticed that the door across the aisle was open—the door to the ship's miniature hospital. Was Terry Allin busy? She had a strong urge to talk to him, to talk to someone, anyone. Moments later, the doctor was beaming his delight that Jody had come to visit him.

In the well-equipped but tiny surgery, Terry leaned against an examining table and said, "Missed you at breakfast, Jody. I had only the ladies from California for company."

"The Westbrooks weren't there, of course," Jody surmised.

"No. Elise is closed up in their suite. I think her husband drank his breakfast on the top deck, alfresco. And the daughter—what's her name—had a tennis date. Sad, isn't it? Mrs. Westbrook just wants her husband's attention. Needs to know that he cares— that's why she faked the appendicitis attack."

"It was that?"

Terry smiled. "She couldn't remember what side her appendix was on."

"I don't understand."

"I'm not being very professional," Terry admitted. "I'm telling you this because it's part of your job to help people enjoy this trip. And that lady could use a warm, understanding somebody to talk with."

"Would it help if I visited her?"

"Without letting her know you're aware of what she did," Terry said.

"I'll have to think of some excuse," Jody frowned. "What?"

"You'll think of something," the doctor assured her. He smiled, his round blue eyes bright with affection. "I'd give you a little more of the patient's background but I have an appointment with the current cruise hypochondriac. There's one every trip. Symptoms of diseases that haven't been invented yet, and invariably healthy as a horse."

Jody laughed. It helped to be around Terry; he made you forget that a few minutes ago you had been all churned up inside.

As Terry was walking her to the door, he changed the subject. "Sorry I was called away last night. I was enjoying our chat in that smoky basement. But you . . . seemed to be able to manage without my company. I expect you know you were the envy of every woman around."

Jody tried to sound noncommittal. "Oh? Neal's interesting enough, yes."

"I read his book." Terry hesitated near the door. "Quite a man-about-town."

"I thought the book was about his famous trials."

"And some of his tribulations," Terry said. "A very frank autobiographical thing. Jody, would I be out of line if I told you to watch your step?"

Jody stared at him in shock. Were her feelings so obvious? "Don't worry, I'm not about to get swept off my feet." She hoped that she sounded convincing. "Actually, Neal can be very smug and irritating. Not my type at all. Although he was . . . flattering enough when he wasn't being aggravating. He told me I'd make a good psychologist, so maybe I'll be able to say the right things to Elise Westbrook after all."

"Oh, I'm sure he couldn't have used that trite old approach. Though it's extremely effective, especially coming from very handsome, successful and popular men. The lady starts believing that she's the only

79

female who can possibly understand him." Terry was shaking his head dolefully as he opened the door. "But I'm sure you're too wise to fall for a line like that."

Jody had felt depressed when she sought out Terry Allin. When she left him, she felt embarrassed, too. How could she have been naive enough to believe everything Neal had said to her the night before? He was a *master* psychologist, an expert at using exactly the most effective word at exactly the right time. She was a fool. Making her way to the Westbrooks' suite, Jody made up her mind to place Neal Rainey in context; an interesting passenger, but just one of many. She had a job to do. The last thing she needed was to get all starry-eyed about a Don Juan whose ego had to be constantly fed, whether on a starlit deck or a sunlit tennis court. If she concentrated on being a real help to Prez, Neal would be erased from her thoughts. She was grateful to Terry for shattering her illusions. And she would let Neal know that she was not as impressed with him as he assumed that she was. She might even, if given the opportunity, make fun of his obvious line, the line he had probably used on hundreds of naive women before.

Jody began her serious effort at being a helpful cruise director in the living room of the Westbrooks' sumptuous quarters. Elise was stretched out on a white velvet chaise lounge, wrapped in a somewhat garish royal blue satin dressing gown. Her eyelids looked swollen, puffy, almost as red as her brightly hennaed hair. She seemed amazed at having a visitor and was extremely apologetic. "I slept late. We . . . entertained last night. I . . . slept late and I'm a mess. You know . . . a little seasick and . . ."

She was extremely nervous and she didn't lie gracefully. A soggy, mangled tissue pressed in her hand, Elise looked as though she might start crying in another second. Surely she realized that almost every passenger aboard ship had been partying in San Juan the night before and that Jody knew this. There were no bottles or glasses on the glass and driftwood cocktail table before her, but the mirrored bar in one corner of the room was well stocked. Jody noticed that the woman's eyes darted in the bar's direction often. She obviously wanted a drink.

Jody decided that her visit needed to be explained. "I'm assistant to the cruise director, as you know, and we . . . we always try to find out about people's interests. That way we can . . . organize our tournaments and classes and . . ." She wasn't doing too well, Jody decided. She launched an enthusiastic description of the craft classes that were available to Elise.

"I'm not talented," Elise said. Her red-rimmed eyes avoided Jody's. "Besides, I wouldn't know what to do with anything I made. Dalton had our house done by a decorator and he wouldn't let me change one thing. And I couldn't give my daughter a present of anything I made. She has such good taste. She's been to . . . to the very best schools. I didn't have her opportunities. I was well along in years before my husband's contracting business became . . . very, very successful."

Jody was concluding that the doctor had been right; Elise Westbrook seemed to be totally insecure and friendless. But she needed to talk and Jody let her go on lauding her beautiful daughter, her enormously successful husband, and her own failings. Finally, she simply ran out of words and said miserably, "I'm afraid you're wasting your time. I'm not really good at . . . anything."

"I think you sell yourself very short," Jody said firmly. "You seem to think of yourself only in terms of your husband and your daughter. I don't mean to interfere, but you're a person in your own right. A very worthwhile person, Mrs. Westbrook. You're . . . for openers, you're a very attractive woman."

It wasn't totally untrue, Jody thought. If the woman got some exercise and took an interest in life, she might slim down, stop hating herself, end the depressing cycle of gin, tears and self-deprecation. If one looked beyond the blowsy effect that had been produced by tears, it was possible to see where Diane had inherited her spectacular beauty. "Wherever did you get the idea," Jody demanded, "that you aren't *somebody?*"

For a few seconds the woman stared at Jody with her mouth agape. And then, as though a dam had been ruptured by an earthquake, she burst into tears.

Jody got up and crossed the room. She pressed Elise's shoulder with one hand. "Sometimes it helps to talk about it, Elise. Even if it's just with a new friend who happens to care."

It took some coaxing on Jody's part, but when the floodgates opened, Elise poured out a story of living with a nice but newly rich man, who let his newfound riches go to his head and spoiled his only child beyond belief, so that when Elise tried to get Diane under control she had no backing from the girl's indulgent father. In Diane's eyes, her mother was the enemy. Her father was the one who loved her, the one who bought her a new Mercedes after she had wrecked her Ferrari. When Diane had been expelled from her third college after a disastrous affair with one of the younger professors, Dalton had comforted his baby with a trip to Europe. And Elise's efforts to keep their daughter off a collision course were met with rebukes. "And I keep making it worse," Elise cried. "Everything I say or do only makes them . . . hate me more!"

"They don't hate you," Jody comforted.

"*Look* at me!" Elise shrilled. "I can't stand the sight of myself in a mirror." She lowered her voice then, still crying softly. "You won't believe this, Jody. But . . . when Dalton married me, I . . . I looked almost exactly like Diane. Oh, a little shorter. I was shy. I . . . didn't have all Diane's . . . verve. But I wasn't the miserable mess I am now."

"Stop that!" Jody was surprised by the firmness of

her command. "You're going to start liking yourself. Tomorrow, you're going to join the yoga and exercise-dance classes. You'll be doing me a favor. My boss wants those classes filled and it's my job to see that they are."

Elise was hesitant, but she didn't seem displeased by being talked to like a willful child. "I might as well be . . . doing something," she sniffed. "I can't stop Diane anyway."

Jody moved back to her chair. "Stop her from what, Elise?"

"Creating another big, ugly scandal." Elise got to her feet unsteadily and crossed the room. She picked up a book from a built-in desk under one of the portholes and returned to hand it to Jody. "Whenever Diane goes after a man, it's like an obsession. And usually, what Diane wants, she gets. This is the . . . newest person on her want-list. A man almost old enough to be her father."

Jody was familiar with the book and with the photograph on its back cover. "Neal Rainey," she said.

"Yes. She's playing tennis with him now. And if I say one word of caution, I'll have Dalton accusing me of . . . being a dictator, spoiling our little girl's fun."

Jody stared at the photograph for a moment. Strange, the way just a picture of Neal could affect her physically. She had studied the studio portrait for a few minutes this morning before she realized that she had slept late and wouldn't have time to start reading Neal's book. But did he pass copies of his best-seller to every woman he met, certain that the descriptions of his outside-the-courtroom life were so tantalizing that they would enhance his already formidable sex appeal? Jody felt sickened by the thought. The humiliation of having believed that she was someone special in Neal's eyes was bad enough. But now, looking at his perfect, strongly masculine features, at his black, boudoir-suggesting eyes, she was seized by a pang of jealousy.

Why? Because a spoiled-rotten teen-ager and an avowed man-about-town were together?

Jody left the Westbrooks' suite shortly afterward. She had gotten Elise to promise that she would splash some cold water on her face, put on fresh makeup and sunglasses to hide her tear-ravaged eyes, and come up on deck where she wouldn't miss one of the high spots on the cruise. "I've read that the entrance into the harbor is like coming into a . . . well, a storybook place. Pastel houses with gabled roofs, the kind you only see in children's books. And a pontoon bridge that moves aside to let the big ships pass. I'll meet you in the observation lounge, Elise. Please don't miss it."

Elise had squeezed Jody's hand and thanked her for being a friend. The word stabbed at Jody. *Friend.* Neal had made it clear that he would never be anything more. If she had responded too heatedly to Neal's kisses and caresses, if she had believed his romantic words, it was only because she was inexperienced and gullible. He had every right to enjoy the company of other women. And if she saw through his line, if she took Terry's warning seriously, maybe she could avoid thinking, behaving, and, yes, *hurting* like a terribly foolish schoolgirl who didn't know the difference between an adoring Adonis and a man on vacation, out for a fling.

Chapter Six

It was a joy to see Elise Westbrook in the glassed-in observation lounge shortly afterward. It was especially gratifying to see that she had made remarkable improvements in her appearance and that she was not alone. Her husband and daughter were with her as the *Caribe Queen* glided majestically into the harbor entrance to Willemstad, the capital of the Netherlands Antilles. Jody avoided the trio; Elise was with her family and didn't need a sympathetic friend.

Prez had assured Jody that she could be most useful by learning as much as she could about the quaint island of Curaçao. And Terry Allin had apologized for not being able to show her the sights because he had a patient suffering from symptoms that might preclude a coronary; he could not possibly leave his hospital. Jody was beginning to feel dejected, expecting to spend the day with a shore excursion of passengers she didn't know when she saw Neal cutting his usual impressive swath through the vast lounge, walking straight toward her. "Where've you been?" he demanded. "I've been calling your cabin, calling the office, looking all over for you. I thought we had a date."

She wanted desperately to pretend that she had forgotten all about that. She wanted to be cool and aloof and indifferent. But looking at Neal now, a pale blue silk shirt unbuttoned almost to his waist, Jamaican-style, revealing his tanned, muscular chest, white slacks immaculately pressed, his square chin enhanced by its intriguing cleft, his dark eyes smiling but shadowed as if with some secret, mysterious knowledge, Jody felt her pulse racing. She had wanted to get back at him, ridiculing his "trite line of patter," but all she could do was stare at him, amazed that he had sought her out. More than that, she wanted to impress Neal, to convince him that she was sprightly and clever and fun to be with. She was comparing herself with Diane Westbrook, she knew. Yet she felt proud and almost superior. Neal may have had a few laughs with the blond beauty after a tennis match, but Neal had taken Jody into his arms. Standing this close to him, she was palpably aware of his lips pressed against hers. He had kissed her longingly and lingeringly. He had called her beautiful. How could she send him away now with some cutting remark?

She couldn't. Thrilled with his nearness, Jody watched the exciting entrance into Willemstad with Neal. They commented on the rows of colorful buildings on either side of the channel, they talked about the incredible blend of African, Indian, Spanish and Dutch cultures that were blended on this arid island. And Neal expressed amazement that Curaçao, home of the famed liqueur, also boasted some of the world's largest oil refineries.

There was an interminable wait before they were able to go ashore; some delay with the port authorities. It was during that time that Neal noticed the Westbrooks clustered around the nearest bar. "The family that drinks martinis together, quibbles together," he said lightly.

Jody smiled. "I think someone's being misquoted."

"But I do feel sorry for Diane," Neal continued, more serious now. "She's a delightful girl when you get her away from her parents. They have the suite next to mine, you know. And thank heaven for soundproof walls. They're forever arguing in the hallway as they come and go. Can you imagine a lovely young girl like that having to be stuck on a long cruise with that bombastic braggard of a father? And that neurotic mother?"

Jody decided not to tell Neal what fed Elise Westbrook's neuroses. Besides, a staff member didn't discuss the passengers with each other. She noted Diane's splashy silk halter-top print; blazing tropical colors against a white background that accentuated her tanned face, arms and beautifully sculptured legs. Her own butter yellow cotton shift looked very plain by comparison, Jody thought. But she was determined not to display her envy. "I take it you've gotten acquainted with Diane." Did she sound casual enough? "She's *so* attractive."

"And fun," Neal commented. "Plays one hell of a game of tennis."

"And always has the good sense to lose?" Jody could have bitten her tongue for the caustic remark. Neal gave her a long, inquiring look and she covered her gaffe by laughing. "I wouldn't have to try. I don't even know which end of the racquet to hold."

Neal laughed, too, saying something about having to remedy that situation. Apparently their laughter caught Diane's attention. Either that, or she had been surreptitiously keeping an eye on Neal all along. Jody's heart sank as she saw Diane crossing the lounge to where Neal and Jody were stationed next to one of the wide, ceiling-high windows.

Diane's smile was dazzling. She nodded at Jody. "Hi, Miss Sommers." Then, assuming a proprietary air, she said, "Are you coming along with our group? We're going to take a bus tour of the island."

"I'm afraid I can't join you," Neal said. "I'm with the party of other attorneys. We've planned our day together as a group."

Jody's disappointment was more than matched by

Diane. "Oh. Oh, I see. Well, another time." Diane acknowledged Jody's presence again. "I suppose you have to stay on board. But you've probably seen Curaçao dozens of times."

Before Diane could be told that this wasn't so, she found it necessary to save face. "Well, I won't lack for company. I've been having a fantastic whirl. But I've got to spend some time with family. I wouldn't want Daddy to change his mind about a shopping spree to end all shopping sprees. Can't pass that up, can I?"

Neal shook his head pleasantly. "Not if you're wise."

If Diane had expected Neal to change his mind and to offer to join her excursion group, she hid her disappointment with the skill of a gifted actress. She flashed another smile at him, gave her magnificent hair a wanton toss and said, "Maybe I'll see you around the island, Neal." She must have been conscious of the stunning picture she made as she crossed the room to rejoin her parents.

"Maybe I'll be in your way," Jody said. "I didn't know you were going on a tour with your lawyer friends."

"Inexcusable falsehood," Neal said in a mock tone of secrecy. "I just didn't want to get mixed up with the whole Westbrook clan. You and I, Jody, aren't going to get herded on any tour bus and told how long we have for lunch. We're going to get lost together again."

It was the beginning of a day straight out of Jody's most delicious daydreams. They walked from the ship to the bustling town, experiencing the thrill of staying on the pontoon bridge as it was moved to parallel the shore to let a large tanker enter the harbor. They avoided the shops crowded with other tourists, strolling the narrow streets and promenades filled with local residents and, quite by accident, ran into some sort of local festival, so specialized that it had not been mentioned in the ship's program. Both regretted not

88

having a camera as youngsters in brilliant costumes paraded to the music of a children's band. Most of the instruments were homemade; the percussion was provided by sticks tapped rhythmically against pots, pans and even the metal portions of garden hoes. But the smiling, dark-skinned children paraded proudly, each step an exuberant dance.

"If we'd gone on a tour, we'd have missed this," Neal said. He pressed Jody's hand. And their hands remained locked even after the excitement of the parade had ended.

It was fun, too, Jody thought, to be mistaken for honeymooners by a gracious vendor along the *Maduro-straat*. "Gentleman wish to buy pretty straw bag for even more pretty wife?" Neal insisted upon buying the embroidered straw bag for Jody. "I liked the man's pitch," he said.

Once, standing on a corner and trying to decide which way to turn, they ran across a group of passengers from the *Caribe Queen*. Oddly, Prez was serving as their tour guide, nervously counting heads and leading them like a flock of chickens. "Observe the colors of the buildings," he said to anyone who cared to listen. "Vanilla, strawberry, raspberry, blueberry frappé and lime sherbet."

After the party had gone on its way, Neal and Jody, still holding hands tightly, made a fun game of naming the building colors after less-fattening foods. "Salmon patties," Jody would say.

"Lox," Neal corrected. He indicated a newly-painted structure done with rose-colored walls, beige window trim and pale green doors. "And that, my dear tourists, is a ham on rye with just a dab of avocado."

They both laughed like children and Neal hugged Jody impulsively. She felt flattered that he had chosen her to spend another day with. More than that, she found herself stealing glances at him as they walked the narrow streets. Just looking at him made her breathless. Holding hands with him gave her a tingling sensation. How would this day end? Would he reach out for her again, explore her mouth with a warm, darting tongue, touch her breasts and tell her he wanted her? And would she be able to remember what Terry had told her?

They were still playing their carefree game and laughing when they came to a charming patio where rum coolers were the specialty of the establishment. It was while they were sipping the tall, icy drinks that Jody learned that she was being escorted by more than a fantastically handsome man. Neal was a celebrity. A middle-aged man, his neck hung with an assortment of cameras, approached their table.

"Excuse me, but . . . aren't you Neal Rainey?"

Reluctantly, it seemed, Neal admitted that he was.

The man turned to his companions at a nearby table. "Didn't I tell you? It's Neal Rainey, all right."

It was the signal for a crowd of American tourists to gather around the table asking for Neal's autograph. He was patiently signing everything from tour maps to cocktail napkins when Jody started thinking that these strangers knew more about Neal's professional and private life than she did. And she was grateful, when they were finally alone, that Neal didn't mention his best-selling book. It would have been embarrassing to admit that she hadn't opened it yet.

"So much for that," he sighed. "Let's go somewhere where there aren't any cruise ship passengers. And when we go to Aruba and Caracas and Martinique, let's go to some secluded beach. Rent a car and get away from other people."

"A beach would be glorious," Jody said.

Neal had reached across the table to take her hand. His eyes, as they locked with Jody's, sent a silent and sensual message that shuddered down her spine. "So you don't play tennis yet," Neal said. "Do you like to swim?"

"I love to." It was one sport at which she excelled.

"Beautiful. I get to see you in a bikini."

Jody met Neal's gaze, happy that she did not flinch before the stare that implied so much. "We're just friends, remember?" she challenged.

"*Close* friends."

Jody shrugged. She was beginning to act more like a woman of the world, she thought.

"Jody?"

"Mmm?"

"Let's have something to ease our hunger pangs. And then let's get back to the ship. Appease a more important hunger. I want to be alone with you. Really alone."

"We could sit at the piano bar," Jody teased. "And talk."

"We've talked enough," Neal said in his sexiest tone.

For a long, exhilarating moment they looked into each other's eyes. "We need to talk a lot more," Jody said quietly. "I don't . . . I don't know anything about you."

"I know one good way for you to learn," Neal told her. He waved for the check and they left the patio soon afterward, Jody conscious of the eyes that followed their departure.

A steel band and limbo dancers imported from Nassau provided the entertainment at the crowded Creole restaurant where they spent the next few hours. They savored a piquant *jambalaya,* washed down with drinks made from a heavy dark local rum that Jody felt going to her head. And then there was another incident with autograph hunters and Neal pleaded, "Let's go back to the ship, Jody. I'm peopled-out. And I want you close to me. As close as you can get."

How could it be possible that he was as attracted to

her as Jody was to him? A wave of anticipation swept over Jody. This man who was the subject of so much adulation wanted, more than anything else, to be alone with her. Remembering his kisses, Jody could think of nothing else but being in his arms once more.

It was nearly dark when they left the restaurant and they were tired from walking all day. Besides, Neal was eager to get back to the *Caribe Queen,* so he hailed a cab. They were getting into the taxi when Jody saw Diane Westbrook standing in front of another restaurant just a few yards down the street, staring in Jody's direction. Neal had been holding Jody with an easy intimacy as they had waited for the cabbie to open the back door, his arm circling her waist. As Jody settled into her seat, she caught only a fleeting glimpse of Diane's face. Under the street lights her green eyes were fixed upon Jody with a look of undisguised venom. The look stayed with Jody throughout the short drive to the ship.

But Neal didn't give her a chance to dwell upon that strangely chilling incident. In a secluded corner booth in one of the ship's smaller lounges, he ordered drinks and then placed his arm over her shoulders, pulling her close. His lips brushed her forehead, then whispered against her ear, "I can't remember a more beautiful day, Jody. Let's make it a beautiful night, too."

"We're . . . having a beautiful night," Jody replied.

"Alone. Please. I'll have the steward bring drinks to my suite. This place is too crowded."

Jody couldn't help smiling. Most of the passengers were still on shore; there were exactly two other people in the lounge, a pair of honeymooners who weren't aware of anyone but each other. "I think I've had enough to drink as it is," Jody said.

"Enough to destroy your inhibitions? I hope so." They were looking at each other closely again, a thrill that Jody found almost unbearable. Then, as Neal's hand drifted down from her shoulder, Jody responded to the electricity of his touch. There was no one else in the lounge; there was no one else in the world except the two of them. Their lips fused in a long kiss, as heady as the drinks that Jody had been sipping. Neal lifted his mouth from hers, but there was that irresistible force drawing them together again. He kissed her again and again, his hands caressing her as intimately as they dared in this public place. "Jody, let's go to my room. I want you. I want to make love to you."

She wanted him, too, though she barely knew what would happen when they were alone. Didn't he know, or should she tell him that no man had ever possessed her, that his kisses had wakened a torrent of desire that she wasn't sure that she could control, didn't *want* to control?

A waiter arrived with their rum drinks, discreetly clearing his throat to give them warning. Neal let Jody go, scowling at the interruption as he signed the tab.

Embarrassed, Jody made a pretense of light conversation. "Aruba tomorrow. I wish I could see it."

The waiter had disappeared into the dark shadows of the lounge before Neal said, "Of course you're going to see it. We're going to have another fantastic day together. If we don't sleep too late." His smile was one of delight and innuendo.

"No, I won't be going ashore this trip," Jody told him. "It's an optional excursion. A plane trip from Curaçao. Didn't you know? A lot of the passengers will be staying on board, and there's a huge party planned for after dinner. Prez will need me."

"I'm going to miss you."

"I'll miss you, too," Jody said. "But I have to keep remembering that I'm not on vacation." She laughed, suddenly feeling giddy. "Can you imagine my being paid for spending this wonderful day with you?"

Neal's dark eyes glowed with a look that was like a

passionate embrace. "Drink up," he said. "You've got to be feeling what I feel now. I can't be separated from you another minute. I've got to have you, Jody. I've got to!"

Her heart pounding an erratic tattoo, Jody was sipping her drink when Neal got up abruptly. He reached down for her hand and pulled Jody to her feet. Somewhere, in another lounge, one of the ship's three orchestras was playing a romantic ballad. It added to Jody's sense of living in a dream, a dream in which she was finding the love for which she had always yearned. Neal wanted her. In another few minutes she would be alone with him, completely alone. And she would pass through the gates which separated her from being a completely realized woman.

They were waiting for the elevator that would take them to Neal's floor, arms around each other's waists, when Jody saw Diane Westbrook again. Diane had changed clothes in record time; she was wearing a pair of skin-tight, flesh-colored disco pants topped with a see-through apricot colored top through which a beige lace bra was plainly visible. She looked radiant and fresh and sexy, making Jody feel rumpled in the yellow cotton she had worn since early morning. And, as always, her radiant smile was directed at Neal. "Hi, stranger. Didn't see much of you on the island today." Jody was patently ignored.

There was an exchange of small talk about Curaçao's many attractions. Then, announcing that she was meeting a date in the discotheque, Diane said, "Going to Aruba tomorrow?"

"I wouldn't miss it," Neal said.

"Lovely." For the first time, Diane honored Jody with a cool glance. "You, too?"

"I'm afraid I'll be working on board tomorrow," Jody said.

Diane's smile returned. A sly, triumphant smile, it seemed to Jody, though that may only have been a reaction to her own resentment. "I'll see you tomorrow, then, Neal."

"Fine," Neal said. "See you tomorrow."

Diane hurried off in the opposite direction. Neal's eyes didn't follow her. He pushed the elevator button impatiently for about the third time.

A sudden weariness crept over Jody as she was reminded that Neal could probably have any woman on the ship that he wanted. Women that were more in his league of sophistication and here she was on the way to his suite and he had arranged . . . "Never mind," Jody heard herself saying.

Neal looked puzzled. "Never mind what?"

"Never mind ringing for the elevator."

Neal reached out to touch her. "Honey, what are you saying? We need each other. We . . ."

Jody jerked away from his touch as she thought, what kind of idiot did he take me for? It wouldn't have made any difference to him tonight if he'd been pouring drinks into me . . . or into some other woman.

Neal looked astounded. "What's come over you, Jody? A few minutes ago . . . I thought . . ."

"You thought I'm too naive to see through your . . ." Jody wavered on her feet. She felt a perverse need to hurt Neal, to let him know that *this* attempt at a conquest had failed. "Your corny line! Oh, you're so obvious that it's pitiful! Telling me that you're lone-ly." Jody dragged out the word, mocking him, adding a derisive sound. "So lonely! And I'm so-o-o understanding. I should be a psychologist, I'm so understanding. And I'm so-o-o beautiful. You can't wait to be alone with me."

Neal was staring at her as though she had gone mad. And maybe she had. She felt foolish and stupid and humiliated. Her head was spinning and the tears that had sprung up in her eyes were tears of anger because she had nearly let herself be used. And suddenly Jody was laughing at him, the way he would have laughed at her tomorrow morning after he had discarded her and turned his attention to his next date, his next ego-boosting victory.

She felt Neal's hands clamp down hard on her shoulders. "Jody, stop that! You're hysterical!" The elevator doors slid open, revealing an empty cubicle. Neal ignored the elevator. He was shaking Jody, looking at her furiously now. "That didn't originate with you! Who told you that was a 'line'? Damn you, Jody, you know I meant every word I said to you last night!"

Jody struggled to free herself from the powerful grip of Neal's hands. "Let go of me! Let go . . . you're hurting me!"

"Whoever told you I was a . . . a hypocrite?" Neal gave her another hard shake that made Jody gasp. He was frightening when he was angry. He was capable of being cruel, capable of hurting her! "You can go back and tell your . . . advisor that every word I said to you was true. I don't have to lie to women. And I'm through having them lie to me!" Neal's hands pressed into her flesh so hard that Jody gave a yelp of pain. His eyes blazed with fury and contempt. "But I think I can take a cheat better than I can take a tease."

"A tease?" Jody shrilled the words. Her voice sounded strange to her own ears. It was like hearing herself shouting from another room. "I haven't . . ."

"You were on your way to my room," Neal snarled. He released his hold on Jody's shoulder, shoving her away from him. "Or you pretended to be. Was that it, Miss Assistant Cruise Director?"

The elevator doors slid shut. Jody tottered on her heels for a moment. And then she was stumbling down the hallway, feeling as though someone had shredded her viscera, as though all the crying and screaming and cursing she could muster would not release the pain she felt inside. Neal made no attempt to follow her. She heard him say, "There's a name for women like you. I'm too polite to use it."

Somehow she managed to get down the stairs to the lowest deck on the *Caribe Queen*. Somehow she managed to unlock her door. But lying across her bed, dry sobs raking her body, there was one thing she could not manage; she could not shut out the memory of Neal Rainey's parting words.

Chapter Seven

Jody didn't waken from a bad dream; she woke up to one. It took only a few seconds to orient herself. The *Caribe Queen* was still anchored in Curaçao. And last night. . . .

Jody shuddered, closing her eyes, wanting to shut out the pain and the shame of the scene she had created with Neal Rainey. He had lavished attention on her all day. He had asked her to fly to Aruba with him—he had asked her *first*. And when he learned that she couldn't go, he had accepted a casual invitation to join another party of passengers, only one of whom happened to be young, beautiful and aggressive.

Her head ached and she knew that if she had not been tired from so many new experiences, so much sightseeing, so little sleep and so many rum coolers, she would have behaved differently. She had never drunk more than a glass of wine with dinner. Last night . . . last night, after an idyllic day with a fascinating man, she had made a complete fool of herself.

Neal's parting words still rankled as Jody got herself together to face the day. A long shower helped. Plunging into work might erase the memory of both the blissful moments she had shared with Neal and the raging, senseless jealousy that had put him out of her life. For there was no doubt in Jody's mind that there would be no more exciting dates, no more kisses, no more invitations to share his love.

She had to forget him. Concentrate on her job before she lost it making an idiot of herself over a man who was too good to be true in one moment and too arrogant and cruel to be bearable in the next.

Fortunately, Prez MacCauley had plenty for her to do. In the office they shared, he gave Jody a long list of matters to be attended to. "Nostalgia Party after dinner tonight for the older married couples," he said. "That's the Benny Goodman set and I'll oversee that. I want you to see that the singles don't miss the disco contest in the Castaways Club."

Jody asked what he wanted done.

"Scurry around the ship between now and dinner, when the passengers who've gone to Aruba will be getting back. Make sure that we have a good turnout."

"We have some honeymooners," Jody pointed out. "Do we promote the couples dance or the singles party?"

Prez scowled. "My dear, one of the least taxing parts of this job is finding something for our honeymooners to do." He handed Jody a key. "This unlocks the storage cabinet at the back of the purser's office. There you'll find the makings for costumes. Fabrics, crepe paper, masks, you name it."

"And?"

"And I'd like you to see that everyone on board comes to the Masked Ball tomorrow night in costume. Many of the passengers come aboard with elaborate getups for the costume party, but a greater number of them don't. You help them improvise and supply them with whatever is needed. In your copious free time, I want you to work with me on setting up a bridge tourney for some of the lawyers' wives. And, since you can't see Aruba this trip, at ten o'clock I'll be giving an orientation lecture in the observation lounge. Drop by if you can. One of these days soon, I'll be turning the lectures over to you."

He added more duties, making up for his neglect of Jody during the past two days. Then he left the office, looking like the Mad Hatter, late to the tea party.

Jody skipped the lecture. Everyone who was going ashore would be there, she suspected. Neal would be there, and she couldn't face him. Yet how long could she go on avoiding him? At dinner, at breakfast tomorrow morning, at the scheduled parties and future shore excursions, it would be almost a full-time job to avoid him. Worst of all, her heart ached with the thought that even if she could manage not to run into him during the rest of this cruise, she would only have made certain that she never saw Neal again.

Jody applied herself to the task of recruiting single passengers for the disco dance and contest, discovering that most of them had read the ship's bulletin and were already planning to attend the gala affair. Going from sundeck to sundeck, lounge to lounge, she worked hard at being the gracious, fun-filled hostess, but the light banter with carefree passengers only served to depress her. She felt desperately out of place and lonely. Yet, only yesterday she had been looked at with envy by most of the women on board.

When she was sure that the excursion party had left the ship, Jody unlocked the costume cabinet, acquainted herself with the materials that would be available, and began another tour of the ship, promoting the Masked Ball.

Her usual table companions, the three ladies from California, had opted to stay on board. They were delighted with Jody's suggestion that they outfit themselves as the Marx brothers; this was going to be more fun than they had had in years. Jody distributed white fabric and silken cord with which to improvise Roman togas, plastic flowers and fruit from which to fashion towering Calypso hats, horror masks for those who chose to appear as movie monsters and even scraped together the makings for an elderly lady who decided that she wanted to appear as Scarlett O'Hara.

Shortly after lunch, where there was open seating because so many of the passengers were ashore, Jody saw Dalton Westbrook at the main bar on the Marine deck. Reluctantly, Jody approached him, reminding him that the next night was going to be exceptionally colorful. Did he and Mrs. Westbrook have costumes?

"I don't worry about things like that," the paunchy contractor said. "Go talk to the wife."

"Elise didn't go ashore, either?"

"Nah. My feeling is, you've seen one island, you've seen them all." Dalton gulped down his drink and waved at the bartender for another. "I work hard for my money. When I want a vacation, I want a vacation, know what I mean? I don't want all that trampin' around some old place where the people don't even speak American, most of them."

Jody was pleased to learn that Dalton's wife was "at some dumb exercise class." He added his usual deprecating remark: "About time, for all the good it'll probably do."

Jody found Elise at the sparsely attended lose-weight-to-music class, conducted by one of the young dancers from the nightly cabaret revue. The session was ending as Jody arrived on the shaded Nautilus deck and Elise, garbed in shorts and a T-shirt, looked perspired but enthusiastic. "Oh, Jody, I really enjoyed this! I'm going to be here every morning, if I have to miss all the sightseeing there is."

But Elise's mood changed somewhat when Jody accompanied her to the Westbrooks' suite to see what Elise had in mind for a costume. "I wanted to go to Aruba," she said, "but Diane said she wanted some space. Do you know what that means? She didn't want her father and me cramping her style. And what really got me is that my husband agreed with her."

Jody refrained from making any comment. The last thing she needed was to get embroiled in the Westbrooks' family squabbles.

Elise shook her head miserably, but Jody was pleased to notice that she didn't walk over to the bar and pour herself a drink. Instead, she pointed at Neal Rainey's book, which now rested on the cocktail table, picture side up. "Diane's going to spend the whole day with *him.*" She nodded at the photograph of Neal. "On some secluded beach, I'm sure. She spent half an hour posing in front of that mirror, trying on different bikinis. And I'm worried."

"I'm sure it will be all right," Jody consoled. She had a mental picture of Neal and Diane together, the two most gorgeous specimens on the beach. Diane wouldn't tease a man. Diane would know what he wanted and see that he wasn't disappointed. Lamely, Jody added, "There'll be lots of people around to chaperone."

Elise gave her a look that said, "Who are you kidding?" Then, as though she was reluctant to reveal too much about her daughter's expertise with men, she said, "I can't help worrying. He's a very sophisticated man. I've been reading his book when I can't sleep at night. And Diane's so young!" She changed the subject suddenly, showing surprising enthusiasm for the costume she had decided upon.

Jody approved a harem costume Elise had bought at a costume shop before leaving home. It was an elaborate, expensive affair covered with beads and spangles.

"And I brought along some gold satin," Elise said as she returned her *houri* getup to the closet. "I hope I can talk Dalton into letting me wrap it around his head, like a turban."

"Perfect!" Jody said. "With maybe one fake jewel in the center."

"Not a fake," Elise told her proudly. From a dresser drawer, which she had to unlock before she opened it,

Elise brought out an enormous gold brooch, its flower shape sparkling with green stones. "Real emeralds, Jody. Dalton bought this for me a long time ago. He always embarrasses me by telling people what he paid for it, but it's my dearest treasure." She smiled wanly. "Makes me remember the good old times."

Jody was getting up to leave when Dalton Westbrook came into the suite, the inevitable drink in his pudgy hand. He scowled at the object in his wife's hand. "How many times have I told you not to flash that thing around? I've got a mind to take it to the purser's office, get it locked in a safe." He turned a fat grin at Jody, saying proudly, "You know what that little trinket set me back, girlie?"

Elise looked uncomfortable. "Oh, Dalton . . . you promised me you wouldn't . . ."

Dalton shrugged and went on to the larger bedroom of the suite. "I work hard for my money, kiddo. I don't mind lettin' people know I take good care of my family."

Jody left the suite after more praise for Elise's ingenuity and went to her cabin. She thought of Neal's phrase; "peopled-out." She wanted to be alone with her thoughts for a few moments, even though her thoughts would only depress her.

She had kicked off her shoes and sunk to the edge of her bed when she saw the silver bud vase and its single red rose on her dresser. The room steward must have put it there during her absence, but who could have sent it?

Jody knew who had sent the single red rose a few moments later when she opened the gift card that lay on her dresser. In a bold masculine scrawl was written:

Dear Jody,
    I should have known that you neither drink nor visit roués in their rooms. It was such a beautiful

*day. Can we have another? And can we just plain
talk tonight? I'll be back around seven. Forgive me
and be my friend.*

> *Kisses,*
> *N.R.*

She touched the velvety red flower with her finger-
tips, tears starting up in her eyes. He was asking for
forgiveness when it was she who had made the scene,
she who had spoiled what had been the most perfect
day in her life. Jody wished that Neal was in his suite so
that she could call him and apologize.

For a long time, looking at the simple but elegant
gift, Jody struggled with her confused emotions. Was
Neal genuinely sorry, or was he merely trying to mend
fences because he couldn't stand losing out and wanted
another chance? Or did he really care about her? Had
he really meant all those words she had ridiculed, was
he really lonely and in need of her affection and
understanding? How could she feel this torn up inside
about a man she had only met? He was still a stranger,
yet last night she had nearly surrendered herself to him,
body and soul. Was she insane to feel this intensity of
emotion about a man who seemed so far beyond her
reach, and was this just a game that he played with
every woman who came into his life?

Question piled upon question, and she knew that she
needed to talk to someone about it—needed help and
advice as desperately as Elise Westbrook had needed it.
Who was there to talk to?

During the afternoon, Jody talked to several groups
of people about the night's events and the masquerade
party that was scheduled for the next evening. Her
mind was not on her job. One minute she was ecstatic
because Neal had sent her a touching gift and a note
that sounded as though he cared. In the next minute,
she was remembering his insulting last remark, the
other times when he had hurt her, the ease with which

he had made the date with Diane at the very time he was escorting Jody to his room.

Jody had to work at dismissing Neal from her mind. He was like a drug to which she had suddenly become addicted; hopelessly addicted. While she chatted with a few of his colleagues and their wives, members of the attorneys' party who had elected not to fly to the other nearby island in the Dutch Antilles, Jody felt a terrible sense of alienation. None of the group had been told by their travel agent that the cruise would include a costume party, nor could they have cared less. They were brittle and witty and rich, having a marvelous time together, exchanging "in" jokes that made Jody feel stupid and left out of their circle.

"I've got it," one of the men said, laughing. "Let's dress as all the judges who have ever ruled against our clients!"

Another of the lawyers echoed the laughter. "That should be fascinating. Neal's going to have to come in his birthday suit. Can anybody here remember the last case he lost?"

They talked about Neal then as though he were some sort of demigod. He was clearly held in awe by all of these people. Jody had the feeling that she could never be a part of Neal's world and that he knew it; he was just amusing himself with her during a vacation that would soon be forgotten. She felt superfluous, even unwelcome in this crowd of Neal's friends, knowing that they were not taking seriously the project that she was promoting, barely aware that she existed.

When the group moved on to an early cocktail party in one of the suites, Jody was left standing alone, thinking that she was as hopelessly naive and out of her element as a teen-ager madly in love with a movie idol.

By five thirty, Jody's confusion and need to talk to someone who might understand drove her to Terry's office, across the aisle from the cruise director's. Terry was busy suturing the thumb of one of the galley helpers, but he said he would phone Jody as soon as he was free.

Jody returned to her cabin, showering and spending an inordinate amount of time on her hair and makeup, satisfied with the fit of the dressy taupe and white-figured pantsuit which had been one of her major wardrobe extravagances. When her telephone rang, she reached for it eagerly, then remembered that Neal couldn't be back aboard yet. It had to be Terry Allin.

It was. And he was more affable than ever. "You came by the hospital," he said. "What can I do for you, Jody?"

She could only be honest with this open, friendly man. "I need to talk to somebody," Jody said.

"I'm your man. And I have an idea." Terry's warm chuckle came through the receiver. "I happen to have a precious bottle of Soave I've been saving for a special occasion. A gift of appreciation from a passenger I advised on what to do about tennis elbow."

"Oh?"

"And I think it would be appropriate to share it with you. So, why don't you swing down to my cabin? We'll just have time to do the wine justice before we head for dinner."

She would have sounded stuffy and prim and overly virtuous if she had questioned the doctor's motives. If she was going to supervise the social lives of sophisti-cated travelers, she was going to have to stop behaving like a prim Sunday school teacher. "Where do I find you, Terry? she asked.

"Number twenty-seven on the Neptune deck. About halfway down the aisle after you've passed the gift shop."

Less than half an hour later, Jody had knocked on the doctor's door. Terry's easygoing manner put her at ease instantly. And his quarters, since they were his permanent home, did not have the sleek austerity of other suites on the ship. There were decorative items that he had purchased at various Caribbean ports of call: a hand-woven area rug to break the monotony of the standard beige carpeting, framed photographs of friends, and almost as many books as one would find in the ship's library.

Terry poured his vintage white wine into thin crystal glasses, explaining that these were his own possessions; souvenirs from the breaking up of his marriage. As they sipped the chilled Soave, he told Terry, briefly and without rancor, that he had been married to a woman who "should never have gotten involved with a doctor." His wife had gotten tired of having dinner parties disrupted because Dr. Allin had been called to a hospital in an emergency. There had been no children and there was no bitterness. But Terry had wanted to leave the town where they had so many mutual friends. He had taken a cruise aboard the *Caribe Queen*, learned that the ship was in need of a physician, and here, two years later, having given up his practice in Atlanta, he was still curing hangovers and the effects of *mal de mer*. Explaining his first encounter with the C.Q. Terry said, "It was a medical seminar. Similar to the legal convention we have going on now."

Somehow, Terry seemed to know that the attorneys' seminar, and one attorney in particular, were the reason for Jody's visit. Halfway through their first glass of wine, Terry said, "You said you needed to talk. I can imagine who the subject of this conversation is going to be."

Jody gave him a wistful half-smile. "Oh, Terry, is it that obvious?"

He nodded sagely. "It is to me. And I've barely seen the two of you together."

Perched gingerly on the edge of Terry's convertible sofa, Jody looked into the doctor's round, totally trustable face and said, "I hope you don't misunderstand. It's not that Neal means anything to me."

"Of course not."

"It's just that . . ." Jody drew a deep breath and released it slowly. "There's got to be some kind of mix-up in time. Like in one of those science-fiction stories you read. I haven't known him for years. It's been just a couple of days. And . . . so much has happened. I don't understand it."

"A cruise ship is a time capsule, Jody," the doctor said. "People are thrown together day and night, for one thing. There's a feeling of being separated from the rest of the world, as though no other place exists. And there are two other factors that may have contributed."

"Yes?"

"One, you're one of the most honest, unpretentious, inexperienced young women I've ever met. Probably an incurable romantic. Yes?"

Jody sipped from her wine and nodded. "I guess."

"And you're dealing with an exceptional man. Physically attractive. Dynamic personality. Famous. A more sophisticated woman could easily get her head turned around. Especially since he appeals to your maternal instincts."

Jody was stunned. "My *what?*"

"Maternal instincts. All women have them. Look, Jody, I read the man's book. He was gentleman enough not to go into detail, but between the lines a reader could gather that he's been hurt. Badly hurt. He knows that he shoulden't be bitter or cynical or condemn all women because the one he loved betrayed his trust. But he's still bound to be wary. Cautious. Not willing to expose himself to an emotional situation where he can get clobbered again." Terry's wide blue eyes took on a thoughtful expression. "That's quite an explosive combination. Tell me what's been happening."

Jody decided that there was no point in pretending that she had no real interest in Neal Rainey. Terry was too astute to be deceived. Besides, hadn't she sought him out for advice? She detailed all of her encounters with Neal, repeating the story of their first meeting, which Terry had already heard, and bringing him up to date. Well—almost. She couldn't bring herself to tell Terry that when she had burst out in a jealous tirade the night before, she and Neal had been on their way to his suite.

"A single red rose in a silver bud vase." Terry drained his glass, shaking his head. "Red roses signifying love, of course. I'll have to remember that."

"Remember that? Why?"

"Because it shows class. Under the circumstances, I'd have sent a huge bouquet." Terry offered to refill Jody's glass. "Nice stuff. More?"

"No more. I think I should have learned last night that I should quit while I'm ahead."

Terry poured more of the smooth wine for himself, then said slowly, "Perhaps you're in love."

"I couldn't. I . . ." Jody stopped. What else would cause this aching feeling under her ribs? Why else would she be looking forward to this evening, to the moment when Neal would return to the ship and call her or seek her out at one of the parties? She set the exquisite crystal glass down on Terry's cocktail table. "I'm not in love, Terry. I'm just . . . I'm just terribly confused."

Terry reached over to pat Jody's hand. "Is this the same young lady who did so much for one of my patients? Elise isn't going around all smiles, but I see a ray of hope. Thanks to you."

"Oh, all she needed, I think, was a friend."

Terry's blue eyes were fixed on Jody's. "We all do, Jody. We all do." His smile was wistful, Jody thought. "And the trick is not to let ourselves think beyond that point. The way I could easily do with you." He laughed shortly. "*If* I weren't a whole lot older and wiser in these matters than you are."

He had told her that she could mean a lot more to him. Without saying that he was lonely, Terry had told her that he could learn to care for her as much more than a friend. But he seemed to know that Jody could not possibly see him as any more. Jody finished her wine. She didn't want to talk about matters of the heart anymore. She led the conversation into a discussion of the Westbrooks, three people who probably loved each other and had somehow lost communication. They talked about islands that Jody hadn't seen yet and laughed about Prez MacCauley's eccentric mannerisms. It was a warm, impersonal exchange, though underneath it all Jody knew that Terry was thinking his own thoughts and she was thinking hers.

Terry looked amazed when he checked his watch. "Do you know what time it is? We're going to miss dinner if we don't get out of here!"

Jody got up, thanking him for the wine and for the understanding.

"You really didn't tell me all that much," the doctor said. "But just enough to make me a little concerned." He pressed Jody's hand as he led her to the door. "This is all very new and probably glamorous and exciting to you, Jody. Don't do what a lot of first-time cruise passengers do."

"What do they do?"

"Confuse the romantic setting with romance. Be careful, little girl. You're much too sweet to get hurt."

They were in the corridor and Terry was locking his door when a group of passengers came walking by on their way to the elevator. Jody recognized them as members of the legal seminar, lawyers and their wives and what Prez called "reasonable facsimiles." Exuberant, fresh from either a private cocktail party or from the shore excursion, they were in a boisterous, jovial mood. Jody smiled at them and said "hi" to a few she had talked with earlier in the day.

And then, like a bolt of lightning out of a clear blue sky, she was looking at Neal Rainey and his dark eyes were staring into hers. Neal stopped short, quickly surveying the scene: Jody coming out of another man's room. Jody unsteady on spike-heeled shoes, even though she had sipped only one glass of wine during a prolonged conversation. She saw his eyes make a quick appraisal, darting from her to Terry Allin and then back to Jody again. She made a weak sound, an attempt at a casual salutation. Terry took his key from the lock and, without noticing Neal, said, "All right, Jody. Let's see what our chefs have come up with."

Jody remained transfixed, as though she had been riveted to the spot. For a terrible, interminable moment Neal looked deeply into her eyes, as though he was probing her conscience. Why did she feel guilty? She wanted to explain that she had only had a friendly conversation with a friend. But any attempt at explanation would only have compounded the guilt she felt, the accusation in Neal's eyes. He was telling her that he had apologized for inviting her to his room because he had realized that she was a naive young innocent. But he had been wrong. He had been terribly wrong.

It was an endless period, frozen in time. And then Neal brushed past her, grim and wordless.

"There's lobster on the menu tonight," Jody heard the doctor saying. He cupped one hand under her elbow to usher her toward the elevator.

She couldn't tell Terry that she didn't want to go to the dining room. She didn't tell him that she had suddenly lost her appetite. Jody walked down the long corridor, dreading an evening in which she would be in the same room with a man who had, once again, closed the door between them.

Chapter Eight

Jody got through the dinner, distracted by the excited chatter of the three women from California who were looking forward to seeing Caracas, Venezuela, the next morning. Elise and Dalton Westbrook, although not likely to be mistaken for a couple on their second honeymoon, were, at least, not arguing, and Jody noticed that Neal Rainey's table was occupied by his colleagues; Diane was nowhere in sight.

Jody saw her later at the singles disco party in the Castaways Club. Introducing people to each other didn't seem to be necessary and the thumping music and flashing lights were hardly suited to Jody's glum mood. One person who certainly did not need the services of a hostess was Diane Westbrook, spectacular in a gold lamé jumpsuit and spike-heeled gold sandals, she was the center of attraction, with a line of men waiting to dance with her.

But Diane didn't seem to be enjoying the party any more than Jody. As Jody was leaving the club, the flashy young blonde stopped her near the doorway. "Not leaving?" Diane purred. She took a gold cigarette case from her sequined evening bag. A white-uniformed ship's officer hastened to provide a light. Out of a plume of smoke, Diane said, "But I suppose you have to be up at the crack of dawn, don't you?"

Jody wondered about the purpose of the conversation; Diane usually ignored her.

"Sorry you had to miss Aruba," Diane went on.

"Neal and I had a fabulous time." She let a sly smile cross her face. "I must have worn him out. He wasn't up to this party."

Jody nodded dumbly. She didn't have to have the hurt rubbed into her. "I'm glad you had fun."

"But I'm sure he would have missed me at dinner. I took a quick nap—recharged my batteries for tonight." Diane's green eyes, heavy with mascara, narrowed. "I say he *would* have missed me at dinner, except that I've been told I won't be seated at his table anymore."

Was this the reason Diane had condescended to talk to a mere employee? "I don't understand," Jody said.

"I don't think changing table arrangements is going to help, though." Diane was virtually sneering now. "Whisking Neal into safer territory isn't going to help. I intend to have breakfast poolside from now on. Or in bed. And dinner wherever we happen to be on shore." Taking a quick, nervous drag from her cigarette, Diane added, "And Neal loves the midnight buffets."

"Everybody does," Jody said curtly. "And I think you should know that I don't make the seating arrangements in the dining room. If you're dissatisfied, talk to the maitre d'."

Diane didn't believe her. She made a deprecating sound, then whirled into the arms of the young officer and said, "Let's dance, darling."

Jody left the disco scene, happy to escape the deafening music and the smoke. Diane had been wrong about the table arrangements, of course, but she had gotten her other points across. But why had she bothered? Only a very insecure person would feel the need to flaunt her success. Either that, or a very vindictive, petty person. Jody had only one thought; to get to her cabin before she started to cry.

She had not gone more than ten yards across the lounge that adjoined the disco club when Jody saw Neal. He had been sitting in one of the settees and apparently watching the doorway from which the wild dance music was still blasting. He was looking directly at Jody as he got to his feet, walking directly toward her.

Jody caught her breath. A day in the sun had deepened his tan. In the white tuxedo and pale blue ruffled shirt he had worn to dinner, he might have stepped from the pages of a movie magazine. But his handsome face was unsmiling and grim.

Jody stopped her walk. She forced the kind of smile Prez affected when talking with passengers and said, "Oh . . . hello. On your way to the singles' dance?"

Neal stood before her, scowling. "I can't stand that ridiculous din. I've been waiting here, hoping you'd get tired of it, too."

"I was tired of it before I went in," Jody said. "Just . . . doing my job." Then, realizing what Neal had said, she asked, "You've been waiting for *me?*"

"Didn't you get my note?"

"Yes, but . . ." Would she ever learn to understand this man? "Oh, I haven't had a chance to thank you for the rose. Do I get to keep the silver vase?"

"Stop making ridiculous conversation!" Neal ordered. "The note asked if we could talk tonight. I got back to the ship and tried calling you everywhere. I even went on a walking tour of this boat. I didn't expect to see you coming out of a man's room."

Jody was able to fix him with a level stare. "If you think I'm going to offer you some sort of explanation, you're wrong. You walked past me as though I wasn't alive."

"I was stunned. And I don't mind telling you it was one hell of a slam to my ego. You turn me down one night. At a time when I wanted you so badly it was like . . . having a knife in my gut. And after you'd agreed to come with me." Neal was seething, his voice stern but tremulous. "Then I spend a night thinking about you, deciding I was wrong. You don't drink, but I ply you with rum, like some heavy out to seduce the innocent young heroine. Then I make a silly date with a juvenile, with you standing right beside me. It was only because you couldn't go to Aruba and I wanted some company. But I understood, later, how that must have sounded to you. All *that*. So I want to make amends. And where do I finally find you? Coming out of the good doctor's bedroom!"

"It was a living room!" Jody cried out. "And I've already told you . . . I'm not going to dignify that insult with an explanation!"

As Jody started to brush past him, Neal grabbed her wrist, spinning her around. "You *do* owe me an explanation!"

"Actually, I don't know what right you have to question what I do!" She struggled to free herself from the vise-like grip. "Let go of me!"

"You're going to listen to me!" Neal demanded.

"Why? Why should I? You don't own me! I don't even know you."

Jody's efforts to get away from him were useless. Neal was powerful and he was furious. "No, I don't own you. And you don't know me. But I rearranged my thinking about women the first time I took you into my arms." Neal's tone was scathing. "Because you were all sweetness and sympathy and empathy and innocence."

Jody made a desperate move, wrenching herself free. "I was a tramp in your eyes the first time you met me," she cried. "I'm a tramp again, because I shared a glass of wine with a . . . with a friend I called on for advice. If you want to go through life thinking every woman on earth is a cheat and a liar and a . . . a . . . something you're too polite to name, that's your problem! You can believe anything you want to about me." She had started to cry, but she didn't care anymore who saw her tears. "You're a hateful stranger and I don't ever want to see you again!"

She was sobbing, trying to get past Neal so that she could run to her cabin. He stood in her way like a formidable wall, his arms reaching out and his hands grasping her arms so fiercely that Jody cried out. The cry was smothered in the violent press of Neal's mouth against hers. Her lips felt bruised, her lungs airless as she fought against the demanding pressure. He wasn't expressing love, but his own fury and frustration, and Jody felt as though she were being punished—violated. And it was impossible to move, pinned hard against a steel-like body that imposed itself against hers.

How dare he hurt her this way? What right did he have to expect her to submit to his mercurial moods? There was only one way to get back at him, because he was too strong to fight. Her only recourse was to hold her body rigid, to keep her lips wooden and unresponsive. He wouldn't ever again have the chance to remind her that she had returned his kisses with an equal ardor. Jody held herself stiff, waiting until Neal's lack of breath would force him to release her.

When he did, Neal was trembling with fury. Or was he shaking with another, less hostile, more deeply felt emotion? Jody was immobilized, even though Neal's arms had slid away from her body. He was staring at her as though his own action had stunned him. And Jody had never seen him look more appealing, more needful.

She should have been running, but Jody didn't move. And suddenly she was sobbing like an injured child. "You think you can do anything you want with me! Whatever happened to . . . just being my friend?"

"Jody!" The hoarse whisper must have come from the depths of Neal's being. "Jody, please forgive me. I don't know what made me do that. I didn't think . . . I still can't believe . . . I'm capable of being insanely jealous."

"Of someone you've only known as long as you've known me?"

Neal pondered that incredible thought for a moment. Then he said softly, "Try to understand, Jody. It isn't you. It's me. And . . . something that happened long before I met you. When you've believed in something . . . believed in love . . . totally trusting . . . and then. . . ." He shook his head, not wanting to reveal any more of his emotional turmoil. "I'm already angry with myself for letting myself care more than I want to care about you. About any woman. Only a fool puts his hand into the fire again once he's been badly burned."

Jody had gotten her tears under control. She wanted to reach out and touch Neal, to tell him that all women were not like the one who had hurt him so deeply. But Neal had placed his arm around her waist and was leading her to the glass doors that opened onto the promenade deck.

"I've waited all day to be alone with you," Neal said as they reached a dark, secluded area where there were no passengers along the rail. "We don't have to go to my room. I just want to be with you, Jody. I want to hold you close and know that you're real."

This time, when Neal took her into his arms, she was not the cold, resisting wall of stone she had tried to be moments earlier. There was the heady, intoxicating effect of the tropical air, laying on her senses like a subtle perfume. There was the pale moonlight and the canopy of black velvet sprinkled with stardust, that indescribably beautiful sky above the Caribbean waters. But more than that, there was the nearness of this man whose virility drew her like a powerful magnet, whose fingers were like flame against her flesh as he caressed her gently and then with a mounting ardor that left Jody weak and trembling. His kisses rained on her face, sensuous and warm; then his mouth closed over hers and left her, once more, with the feeling of being utterly possessed, completely his.

If Neal had asked her to his quarters, Jody knew, she would have gone with him, frightened but eager to know him as closely as a woman can know a man. But he did not. Was he thinking that he would drive her

117

away if he repeated his invitation of the night before? That had to be, for there was no doubt that he wanted her. Pressed against his body so tightly that a thin sheet of paper could not have been wedged between them, there was no mistaking his desire, and the knowledge of that desire was like fire in Jody's veins.

They lingered in their almost dark hideaway by the rail until long past the time when other passengers had gorged themselves on lobster thermidor and roulades of veal and caviar at the midnight buffet. And when Neal saw Jody to her cabin door, his black-as-midnight eyes looked at her with an almost worshipful expression as he said, "Tomorrow, Jody. I'll be waiting for you again tomorrow."

Then he was gone so suddenly that it seemed to Jody he had not been crushing her against him only minutes before. And long afterward, lulled by the gentle motion of the ship, Jody recalled the tenderness and the passion she had aroused in this man with whom it would be so easy to fall in love. So easy, she thought, and so dangerous. She *had* to keep him in perspective, Jody reminded herself. She must keep remembering Terry Allin's warnings. Could she simply have fun with him, see the islands with him, revel in the envious glances of other women, and then forget him the way he would probably forget her when this cruise ended? She would have to try. She could not let herself fall in love with this impossible dream of a man. She would have to stop remembering, as she was remembering now while waiting for sleep, the thrill of being filled with a raging need for his body as he held her in his arms.

Chapter Nine

In the week that followed, Jody didn't stop to analyze or to try to control her emotions. Neal was at her side every moment that she could spare from her increasingly busy work schedule, every moment that he could gracefully get away from his colleagues.

Getting acquainted with the Caribbean islands would have been exciting enough for Jody. But seeing these exotic never-never lands with her hand pressed tightly in Neal's was a thrill beyond belief. If he was still playing tennis with Diane in the morning, while Jody worked with Prez, Neal didn't mention the fact.

Together, they toured both the Dutch and French sections of St. Martin. A rented car whisked them to secluded beaches where they escaped the other sightseeing tourists, where Jody enjoyed the ego trip of having Neal admire her slender, curvaceous body in a bikini and where, when they swam together and he held her against his near-nakedness in the sun-warmed sea, their kisses grew in intensity, reaching a dangerous ardor.

Then there was the island paradise of Antigua, a blue and gold and white dream that boasted one gleaming sandy beach for every day in the year, and where Jody's first experience with a mask and snorkel tube left her breathless with awe. She was proud of her ease underwater as they explored the coral reefs teeming with bizarre and brilliantly colored fish. Antigua might be only a shopper's paradise to the other *Caribe Queen* passengers. To Jody it was an Eden where Neal found excuses to touch Jody's bare shoulders as he adjusted her mask, where he reached out to run his fingers down her thigh as they floated over the coral grottoes and where they splashed through the surf on a beach so isolated that they both tingled with the awareness that no one would see them, no matter what they chose to do. And it was on one of those remote beaches that they ended a long, laughing race through the ribbon of foam that caressed the firmly packed sand, falling down breathless and exhausted but still laughing, until Jody's laughter was stilled by a hard, bruising kiss from the most exciting man she had ever known.

They had clung to each other for a long time after that, lost in a rapture that set Jody's pulse hammering. Waves washed over their feet in a steady rhythm that was like the pounding of Neal's heart as he pressed his perfect body, warm and wet with salt water, closer and closer to Jody's.

How could Neal have meant it when he had told her that he wanted no emotional complications in his life? Or was this hunger only a temporary physical need? Surely he sensed what Jody knew in her heart; there was an attraction between them that went far beyond their purely sensuous need to hold each other, kiss each other, revel in the pure physical joys that were enhanced here by the penetrating kisses of the sun against their nearly bare bodies.

If Neal had felt the same compelling urges that had engulfed Jody during the breathless time that they lay entwined in each other's arms, he seemed determined, for some perverse reasons of his own, not to let their rapport sweep him too far. He could have made love to her, Jody thought later. He must have known that she was burning with desire for him and would not have been capable of resisting him. But, strangely, Neal let her go as suddenly as he had swept her into his embrace. He stood up, brushed the sand from his chest and his arms, then pulled Jody to her feet. Holding her hand, he resumed their hurried run along the sand. When they stopped running this time, Jody's panting breath was from exertion. Yet she had been breathing just as hard while they had lain together at the water's edge and Neal's hands had slipped beneath the flimsy bikini top, finding her breasts, his fingers bringing a firm response from her nipples. Never before! Never had she come closer to surrendering herself completely. Yet Neal had let her go. Why?

He was enigmatic. Back aboard the *Caribe Queen* that night, either because the encounter on the beach had meant nothing to him, or because he was afraid of learning to care too much, he showed his independence by escorting a woman lawyer in his group to the night's Gay Nineties party. True, it was an event that had been planned exclusively for the attorneys; other passengers were enjoying Monte Carlo Night in the ship's casino. But he could have invited Jody as his guest; she could have been present in line with her duties as Prez's assistant. But Neal didn't even suggest that Jody come to the party, though when they had been together earlier he had made Jody feel like the most beautiful, most desirable woman in the world. She felt cheated, even senselessly jealous.

Jody couldn't help wondering what life would be like if Neal overcame his dread of emotional involvement. What if he did the impossible and asked Jody to spend the rest of her life with him? It would be a hellish torment, Jody decided. So many women wanted him that his wife would have to endure an agony of constant jealousy, constant insecurity. Have fun with him, she kept lecturing herself. Enjoy his attention while it lasts, but don't mistake this romantic whirl for love!

One morning, proofreading the activities bulletin in Prez's office, Jody had these warnings emphasized by Terry Allin. He stood in the doorway, across the hallway from his clinic, shaking his head dolefully, his round blue eyes clouded with concern. "Haven't seen much of you. You've been having quite a go with the Clarence Darrow of the cruise ship set."

"Just . . . seeing the islands," Jody replied, her denial too lame to be believable. "Nothing serious, Doctor."

Terry came closer to the desk. "Look at me, Jody."

Jody felt his eyes searching her very soul. Her eyes met Terry's and she knew that a rush of blood had turned her face scarlet.

Terry's hand touched Jody's shoulder lightly. His eyes studied Jody's face as though he might be inspecting a virus under a microscope, searching for the clues from which he might form a diagnosis. "You've answered my question," he said quietly. "I wish I could say I'm happy for you."

"I'm just . . . having a good time," Jody protested. But those words, too, came out sounding hollow. "What are you so worried about?"

"I'm very fond of you, Jody," the doctor said as he turned away and walked toward the open doorway. "I hope you don't think I'm being envious, though I'd be a hypocrite if I told you I'm not. But I've been around long enough to know that we can't manufacture emotions." In the doorway, Terry stopped and turned, his expression pained. "When I first met you, I had hoped . . . I had thought maybe . . ."

Jody felt her eyes misting. She was enormously fond of this kind, sincere man. But she would not patronize him by pretending that she felt anything for him but a sisterly warmth. "Nothing's changed," she said firmly. "We're going to be good friends, Terry."

He nodded glumly. "After Mr. Rainey gets off the ship. But when that happens, how are *you* going to feel? If you could look at him unemotionally, without stars in your eyes, you'd know what I'm talking about.

And why I'm worried. But you can't do that anymore, can you? And nothing I can say is going to change that."

He was actually feeling sorry for her! Jody slammed her ball-point pen down on the desk, suddenly irritated. "I don't know why you're assuming that I'm going to get badly hurt, Doctor! That's implying that I'm not good enough for Neal Rainey."

"I didn't say that," Terry protested. "If anything, I think you're too . . ."

"Too sweet and naive and innocent?" Jody taunted. She tried to sound like an experienced woman of the world. "Just because Neal and I come from different worlds doesn't mean that we can't . . . we can't . . ." She stopped short of saying that it was quite possible for Neal and herself to fall in love with each other. But the word "love" would have sounded ludicrous, she knew. And Terry's blue eyes were fixed on her face with a knowing, saddened expression. Yes, he was feeling sorry for her. And maybe all those smart, sophisticated women whose envious glances had inflated her ego were feeling sorry for her, too, knowing that Neal had enjoyed flings before and would enjoy them again. Why, he had even been confident enough to warn her in advance that he would not take her seriously!

She was furious with Terry for having pinpointed what was probably the truth, for having placed her heart under his microscope and accurately read her symptoms. It angered Jody to be thought of as a blind little fool, swept off her feet by a handsome playboy with a smooth line and the techniques needed to arouse latent passions in much more experienced women. She felt an overwhelming need to strike back at Terry. "All right, so he's a celebrity and he's ridiculously good-looking and he's . . . he's from a prominent family . . . and he's disgustingly wealthy. That doesn't make me a little nothing." Jody tossed her head back defiantly.

Terry stood in the doorway for one more interminable second and then he said, "I should have minded my own business, Jody. You have my apologies."

He had crossed the hall before Jody could retract her barbed comments.

Jody finished her work feeling sick inside. Terry hadn't deserved that vicious attack. Disgusted with herself, Jody decided that she was not up to dressing for dinner that night. The two evening gowns were beginning to feel dowdy, and she knew it was only because Diane Westbrook made her entrance into the dining room wearing a different designer creation every night. And it had been mention of Diane that had triggered Jody's fury with Elise. Jealous! What right did she have to be jealous?

Every right, Jody told herself grimly. Neal had been monopolizing her time, her mind, her emotions. Only his erratic way of drawing back at the height of her passionate response had kept him from taking possession of her body, too.

At four o'clock, her insides still churning, Jody asked Prez if he would mind if she went to her cabin for a rest. "I don't think I'll be up to dinner tonight," she said.

"My dear, the mood you're in, I don't want you around our passengers," Prez told her bluntly. "You've been pushing too hard and you're on edge. Get some rest."

Jody nodded dumbly. She was physically tired, but it was emotional confusion that was really taking its toll.

"But don't starve yourself," Prez added, more sympathetic now. "Tea's about to be served. Take a platter of little sandwiches and scones and what-have-you to your cabin. Relax. We don't want you looking dreary."

It was a reasonably tactful way of telling Jody that she looked terrible. Later, surveying herself in the mirror, Jody had to admit that her exhaustion was plainly visible. How did Diane keep up with the endless partying, dancing, sightseeing and sports activities?

Tennis. Diane could dance away the night and be bright and perky on the tennis court, keeping her morning rendezvous with Neal.

It seemed that every thought that came into Jody's mind would eventually twist around and come back to Neal Rainey. She altered between an unreasoning anger with him (for, after all, what had he done to trigger this vile mood?) and a yearning to have him beside her. Jody toyed with the "high tea" sandwiches, showered, longed for a huge tub in which to soak away her tiredness and almost laughed out loud at the thought that she was viewing herself as an aching old lady. All she needed was sleep.

Jody took Neal's book from her bedside table and decided to read until she felt her eyes closing. Instead, she found herself staring at his photograph, her fingers running over the pictured face, outlining his strong chin, touching his lips and recalling the searing heat of his kisses. He was busy with his lawyer friends today, but he had promised to call her in the morning. Would he? She could never be sure of him. He'd promised to teach her to play tennis, too, but he hadn't gotten around to it. Too busy playing with a beautiful blonde who offered him a real challenge. *Why* did he keep creeping into her mind, permeating her thoughts, leaving her body damp and warm with perspiration when she had just stepped out of the shower and the room was comfortably air-conditioned?

Jody found herself rereading the story of one of Neal's most celebrated trials. She flipped the pages, looking for more personal anecdotes. The words blurred before her eyes. Jody let the book drop from her hands and sleep enveloped her like a soft black curtain.

Jody woke to the ringing of the telephone. And, yes, it was Neal. He sounded fresh, enthusiastic, totally unaware of the havoc he had created inside Jody.

"Come up on the main observation deck and see the most beautiful sight you've ever seen in your life," he was saying. "We'll have breakfast and then we'll go ashore for a great day!"

Jody dressed in her aqua shirtmaker cotton, the only outfit she hadn't yet worn during the cruise. She tied a jaunty yellow and white silk scarf at her throat, ran a brush through her short unruly amber hair. For one second she wished that it were a long blond flowing mane, but then she decided to like herself again. Yesterday's miseries were a combination of physical tiredness and oversensitivity. Neal had just phoned her. She would be spending another glorious day with him. Maybe she shouldn't be feeling all fluttery inside, excited as a schoolgirl going to her first big dance, but she did, and she wasn't going to let anyone's dire warnings interfere with the joy of this moment. And her heart was still fluttering when she met Neal above deck. In the bright morning sunshine he looked dazzling, his smile radiant, his walk toward her a confident stride, his blue paisley sport shirt open to reveal the bronzed, powerful chest that never failed to make Jody want to be held against it.

They chatted easily during breakfast beside the swimming pool, Neal waving to friends but not inviting them to join him. He made it clear that this was his day with Jody and Jody alone.

And then Martinique! Was there another place in the world like Martinique? Jody wondered.

"Paris," Neal said. "Four thousand miles from the Eiffel Tower, but we may as well be in France."

They shopped for local handicrafts, drove a rented car to St. Pierre, where Mt. Pelée had buried a town under volcanic ash; they relived the romance of Napoleon and Josephine, reminded that the empress had called this island her home. Before lunch in a charming Creole bistro, they stopped in a quaint gallery and bought small Gaugin prints, Jody learning that the

126

artist had painted in Martinique before settling in Papeete. Late in the afternoon, they found one of those idyllic beaches straight out of a travel brochure, totally isolated from the mundane world. They walked along the silver strand until their legs ached, carefree in only bikini and trunks, Jody happier than she had ever remembered being.

There was a provocative few minutes when Neal, worried that Jody was getting too much sun, applied tanning lotion to her back, her arms, then her legs. They didn't speak during this slow ritual, but Neal's caressing hands spoke a language all their own as they smoothed the lotion over her bare skin. Jody tried to relax, but the tension building up inside her threatened to explode.

When he was finished, Neal grinned and said, "Turnabout's fair play." He held the tanning lotion out to Jody, then turned over to lie on his stomach.

Jody caught her breath. Hesitantly, she said, "You . . . probably don't need this, Neal. You're so dark already, you . . ."

"I need this," Neal murmured. His tone was heavy with implications that had nothing to do with avoiding sunburn.

His body was magnificent, Jody thought. She ran her fingers over his back and shoulders, wishing that her hands would remain steady. Touching him this intimately was exciting, but it was almost unbearable at the same time. She couldn't believe that a few short weeks ago Neal had been an awe-inspiring stranger and now she was massaging his firm back muscles, telling him with her fingers that she cared . . . cared far more about him than she wanted to. She thought of Terry's warnings and his concern for her, frightened by the thought that this was just an amusing game with Neal. Was she just a temporary plaything? Was there another betting pool on the ship, where passengers, besides wagering on how many knots the ship would cover in a twenty-four-hour period, also bet on how long it would take a pitiable, naive little fool to realize that a man like Neal Rainey couldn't possibly fall in love with her?

Was it that concern that made Jody spoil the pleasant getting-to-know-each-other conversation that followed? And why did she regress to that needing-to-hurt-before-I-get-hurt stage that Neal understood all too well? Was it because Neal was being affable and fun, even sexy by implication, but so far today had made no attempt to kiss her or put his arms around her?

They were talking about Neal's book, and the state he was in while he was writing it. "I should have taken this vacation right after the Washburn trial," Neal said, stretching his lean body out on the sand. "I'd have realized that the whole world doesn't revolve around my briefs and trials. The ocean keeps beating against the shore. The sun keeps shining down on the palm trees and shells keep washing up on the beach. Eternal things help you put all your own petty little concerns into perspective."

Jody agreed. "But if you'd taken this cruise, then I wouldn't have met you."

Neal's hand reached out to brush Jody's affectionately. "And I wouldn't have met you. But you know what I mean. I was exhausting myself, thinking there wasn't another world except the one I was embroiled in."

Without admitting that she had only read scattered paragraphs of Neal's best-seller, Jody expressed an understanding of the torment Neal must have been enduring during the trial of a young man he believed to be falsely accused of murder. The circumstantial evidence against his client was formidable; he had to face the young man's mother daily without being able to offer her any hope of her son's acquittal. Or so Jody had read. What made her ask the perverse question? "Did you really think you wouldn't win that case? Or did you make it all sound so threatening because . . . well, you know. For dramatic effect?"

Neal turned to look at Jody with a dark frown. "I *was* up against impossible odds."

"But you made the most of that in your book. I suppose it makes a triumph all the more impressive when you've convinced people that you're facing defeat."

Neal pulled himself to a sitting position. His muscles had tensed; he scowled, his dark eyes narrowing. "Is that the way I came off to you? As though I was trying to make excuses for myself, dramatize my brilliance as a trial lawyer?"

He had barely touched Jody today. He hadn't reached out for her here on this deserted beach, hadn't even tried to kiss her. Jody felt neglected and belittled, Terry's words drumming in her mind. "Well, you weren't exactly modest. You set yourself up to become a big hero who overcomes tremendous obstacles."

"Were you pleased with the outcome of that trial?" Neal asked tersely. "How did you feel about the end result, Jody?"

She felt as though she had ventured out on thin ice. Uncomfortable now, Jody said, "Oh, I knew how the trial would end, of course."

"Me triumphant, my innocent client acquitted, the press and all my colleagues hailing me as a hero in the fight for justice?"

Something snide and sarcastic in Neal's voice made Jody very unsure of her ground, but she was driven by an urge to let Neal know that she was not some blind little fool who adored him too much to be critical of his flaws. She wasn't really attacking Neal's ego; Jody was protecting her own when she said, "Let's face it, Neal. You always come out on top, don't you? You know how to manipulate judges and juries. You know how to make people like you—*love* you, when you want them to. It's a talent you've developed. It's an art."

Neal looked appalled. "You've just given me the classic description of a user!" Neal got to his feet. He reached down to pick up his beach towel, walking a few yards away to shake the sand out of it. Then he came back to Jody's side, slipping his feet into his sandals, putting his sport shirt over his arm.

Jody knew that it would be useless to try erasing her accusatory words. She hadn't meant them to sound so harsh. What *had* she meant? Only to let Neal know that she *was* good enough for him because he wasn't some god who had just stepped down from Mount Olympus. She knew that he was angry. To save face, she pretended to ask her question casually; "Time to get back to the ship?"

It wasn't time. It would be another hour before the sun set and they weren't due on board until half an hour before the midnight sailing time. "I think it's way *past* time," Neal muttered. He stood by silently while Jody gathered up her belongings. He was wordless and grim as they walked back to where he had parked their rented car.

Several times, as they made their way back to the dock, Jody started to confess that she hadn't really read Neal's book carefully. But the right words wouldn't come. Neal made a few desultory comments about the crowds of cruise ship passengers who thronged the streets, the cool expertise of the taxi driver. Aboard the *Caribe Queen,* he escorted Jody only as far as the nearest elevator. His polite, "Enjoy your evening," might have been said by a shop clerk in one of the ship's boutiques.

Except to help Prez with arrangements for a bridge tournament the next day, Jody remained alone for the rest of the evening. She cooped herself up in her cabin, sick at heart and despising herself for making a cold, uninformed, insulting judgment of Neal. No man had ever done more to make her happy. Whatever his personality traits, he hadn't deserved to be called a user. And his aloof manner had told Jody more plainly than words that he would not be seeking her company again.

Her radio was playing soft, sentimental music. Jody clicked it off, knowing that if she kept listening she would dissolve in tears. She thought of reading Neal's book, really reading every word, if only to find out why he had taken such sharp offense with her remarks. But reading Neal's words was no way to wipe him out of her consciousness. She was afraid; afraid of falling too deeply in love with him, of knowing the bitterness of rejection, of being humiliated before everyone aboard the ship. For if Terry Allin saw that she was much too fond of Neal, then everyone must be seeing it, too.

In another ten days Neal would be leaving the ship and she would have no choice but to forget him. Maybe he had not kissed her today because he was preparing her for the inevitable; he was being kind to poor, foolish, romance-starved Jody. The time to start forgetting him was right now.

Jody was still working on that seemingly hopeless project when the *Caribe Queen* blasted a farewell to Martinique and slipped out to sea.

Chapter Ten

Fortunately, Prez MacCauley found plenty for Jody to do in the days that followed. Not hearing from Neal, going out of her way to avoid seeing him, Jody busied herself with the many aspects of her new job. She filled out requisitions for playing cards, paperback books and party favors. She worked with the purser, arranging special shore excursions for the golfing enthusiasts who would make up most of the passenger list on the next cruise. There were parties to plan for the arts-and-crafts teachers who were aboard now, public rooms to be cleared for the attorneys' seminar, decorations to be checked for the Captain's Farewell Party on their last night at sea.

Working and learning what would be expected of her was Jody's salvation. If she stayed busy, she would have less time to think about Neal Rainey. But she couldn't stay busy enough. His face was before her day and night. She even wondered if she had only imagined those moments when his arms held her tenderly and then tightened in a fierce embrace, as though he could never hold her close enough against his strong body. Had she really rubbed his back with tanning lotion, hearing him sigh with pleasure as her fingers moved along his deeply sun-bronzed flesh?

It would have been better if she could have remained in the cruise director's office all day, but Jody's varied duties took her to all parts of the ship. She could avoid

Neal in the dining room; there were alfresco meals served elsewhere at almost all hours of the day. But she could not avoid seeing that Neal had turned his attention to Diane Westbrook.

Jody saw Neal and Diane playing tennis in the morning, laughing and talking afterward, Diane's arm slipped possessively through Neal's as they walked to the bar together after their game. Jody was with a rather dull group of passengers on Guadeloupe island when Neal and Diane walked into the bistro that had been chosen for dinner. Their tans had deepened, probably from a long afternoon on one of the beaches that was the pride of this Riviera of the Caribbean. It was painful to remember the times Jody had splashed along the edge of other beaches with Neal. Even more painful was the compliment paid by one of Jody's dinner companions when Neal and Diane stepped out on the dance floor after their meal: "Don't they make a beautiful couple? A man that handsome can pick and choose, I suppose. And he certainly chose a beauty!"

There was one thing to be grateful for. Terry Allin accepted Jody's apology and understood why she had been so unfair to him. "We all get a little edgy at times," the doctor said.

"Especially when somebody tells us a truth we don't want to hear," Jody told him.

The doctor dismissed further discussion of the subject with a wave of his hand. He would settle for being Jody's friend, Terry implied. And, as friends, they would visit the rest of the islands on the *Caribe Queen*'s itinerary together.

With the doctor serving as her escort, Jody was at least saved the humiliation of being with the other unescorted women when Neal saw her leaving the ship on a shore excursion, when he and Diane ran into her in one of the duty-free shops, or in one of the superb restaurants that dot the French Caribbean. Jody's pride was being saved. She had the full attention of the most distinguished and eligible member of the ship's professional staff.

But "saving face" was not enough. On the occasions when Jody found it impossible to stay out of Neal's way, his penetrating eyes stared into her with an expression that would haunt her for hours afterward. He was coldly proper, making it clear that Jody was just another of the passengers with whom he exchanged brief small talk, people one was civilized with, but strangers still; one would never see them again once the ship returned to its home port. Yet, in spite of that aloof manner, Jody was overwhelmed by those accidental meetings. She could not free herself, glimpsing his powerfully masculine chest, of the memory of being held close to him. She would cast her eyes down, not looking at his face. But when she was alone in her cabin at night, Neal's face would be before her, smiling, scowling, sensuous, always a study in male perfection. And now Diane was always beside him, clinging to Neal's arm, teasing him, laughing and looking up at him with an adoration that must be gratifying to Neal's ego. Jealousy raked Jody's mind and body. And she was furious with herself for driving Neal away, frustrated by the thought that he had said he wanted her and she had spoiled it all with a few barely-thought-out words.

Although she tried to hide her feelings from Terry, her misery did not go unnoticed. One evening at the piano bar aboard ship, Terry had watched Neal and Diane chatting in a corner booth across the room and, patting Jody's hand lightly, he said, "Don't let them bother you. They're collectors, both of them. They probably deserve each other."

"Why would they bother me?" Jody asked, shrugging her shoulders with a faked indifference. She knew why. Worse, she knew that Terry did, too.

It seemed that there were reminders of Neal everywhere. Elise Westbrook had invited Jody to the suite for a specially catered late lunch of Mandarin shrimp crepes and icy Margaritas, and she seemed to be in reasonably good spirits. Still, she confessed that she was still troubled by the other two members of her family.

"Where are they?" Jody asked. The ship was at sea, so they had to be somewhere aboard.

Elise pretended to smile as though it didn't matter where they were. "Oh, I'm sure Dalton's found some flashy widow to make a fuss over him at one of the bars. And Diane? She only stops in to change clothes between dates with our famous next-door neighbor. Jody, I've never seen her so tenacious. When she goes out in pursuit of a man, the world could stop turning and she wouldn't notice it."

Jody felt as though someone had stabbed her heart with an ice pick. Lamely, she said, "Then your daughter's having a good time. That *is* what you wanted for her when you booked the cruise."

"Yes, I want her to be happy," Elise agreed. "But I do wish she'd gotten involved with someone closer to her own age. Now, my husband's convinced that Mr. Rainey will have a settling effect on Diane. Dalton's very impressed by educated men with money, you know. He's very conscious that his people were dirt-poor farmers." Elise thought for a moment and then added, "He may be right. Diane could do a lot worse than to marry a man of Neal Rainey's status and good sense. She might just start behaving like an adult."

Jody wished she had not let the conversation about Neal get started. She hoped that her envy wasn't obvious when she asked, "Is it that . . . serious? You think Mr. Rainey is . . . has he asked Diane to . . . *marry* him?"

"I don't know." Elise sighed. "She's never confided in me. But they seem to be spending every waking hour together. It's beginning to look . . . quite serious, though I can't say that the man has been especially cordial to Diane's father or to me. And I've never seen Diane more determined to have a man all to herself."

Elise went on, after that, with a giddy reminiscence of the days when she looked like her stunning daughter and men were throwing themselves at her feet. That reminded her of her new regimen: "Thanks to you, Jody, I'm not just standing up for my rights, but I'm starting to care about my appearance, too. I'll keep up the dance-exercise classes when I get home. And I'll send you a snapshot. You won't know it's me."

Elise had gone from that to a recital of her daughter's successes with men, a reminder that made the rest of the luncheon an anguish-filled experience for Jody. She was glad to escape, pleading a heavy work load in the office.

There was another hurtful reminder later that afternoon when Jody found herself trapped in one of the lounges with Elise's husband. Dalton insisted upon buying a drink for Jody and she was forced to listen to him brag about all that his money had done for his glamorous daughter.

"Diane's got a closet full of these expensive designer clothes, right? Bought some of them in Paris, no less, while I had her in this fancy school there. Brought three trunks full of clothes on this tub." Dalton grinned with satisfaction. "But does she have anything to wear for the captain's big bash? No, siree! On that island . . . what do they call it? Guad-a-loopy . . . she ropes me into this spiffy place where this French lady makes evening gowns to order. They got the kid's measurements and you know what? They're gonna fly this fancy white gown to St. Thomas when it's finished. White, all covered with flowers made out of little white beads, all sewed on by hand. Tell me, is my kid gonna bowl 'em over, or is she gonna bowl 'em over?"

Jody visualized how she would look by contrast. Her two formals were beginning to look so tired that even if she hadn't been avoiding Neal, she would have stayed away from dress-up nights in the dining room. She said something about being sure that Diane would look very lovely, as always.

"Got to," Dalton said. He took a long swallow of Scotch on the Rocks. "You know who my baby's got on the line, all ready to reel in? Biggest lawyer in the whole U.S.A. Wrote this big book, too. I don't go in for books. Too busy makin' money. But can you imagine my little girl gettin' her hooks into somebody that rich and famous?"

Jody was beginning to be able to imagine it. She knew, furthermore, that Dalton's boasting had a double edge. He had seen Jody with Neal too many times not to know that they had been "a shipboard item." There were passengers who had nothing better to do than lie back in their deck chairs and observe the developing romances. Everyone was probably talking about the new staff member who had been discarded by *the* Neal Rainey in favor of Dalton's gorgeous blond daughter. It must have been satisfying to him to let Jody know that. And the humiliation was only a small part of Jody's pain.

Later, looking at her comparatively meager wardrobe, Jody began to dread the gala last night at sea. She visualized herself wearing one of her two Old Faithfuls, watching as Diane made her entrance in a gown that had cost more than Jody would earn in the next two months. Diane was always startlingly beautiful; in a white beaded gown she would be a spectacular vision. Her tan deepened by afternoons on Caribbean beaches with Neal, she would make him proud that he was her escort to the most elaborate dinner party of the cruise. He might have been embarrassed to walk into the room with me, Jody thought dismally.

She didn't tell Terry about her feeling that she was totally outclassed by Diane Westbrook, but she did tell him about the conversation with Dalton. "And, of course, he had to tell me what he'd paid for that custom-made gown."

"Of course." Terry shook his head from side to side slowly. "Maybe it gives him a sense of importance to know that he can spoil his kid."

"And she does have marvelous taste."

"In clothes," Terry said pointedly. "In people, I'm not so sure."

Jody didn't comment. Terry was only reminding her that she was much better off without Neal Rainey leading her on to heartbreak. What she couldn't bring herself to tell Terry was the truth; Neal rarely left her thoughts. The sight of him made her heart leap. When she closed her cabin door behind her at night, she could think of nothing but the ecstasy she had felt with Neal's lips pressed against hers, her crying need to be held by him, touched by him, loved by him.

How could she have fallen this desperately in love so fast? It was because the outside world was shut off aboard the *Caribe Queen*. The ship was a microcosm, with years packed into weeks, hours stretching out into days. People saw each other at close hand every day and every night, so that the pace of relationships was accelerated. She felt that she had loved Neal Rainey all of her life. And Jody could scarcely remember a time when Dr. Allin was not at her side, always sympathetic, almost worshipful, sometimes looking at her with an expression that worried her. He was too fine a man to be encouraged. Yes, it would be wonderful if she could return his affection, but Jody knew that she could not learn to love him. Not the way he wanted to be loved, not the way she loved Neal; heart, body and soul.

How agonizing it was to know that Neal would be exploring St. Thomas, their first port of call in the Virgin Islands, with Diane! Seeing Charlotte Amalie, the island's capital, with Terry would be pleasant, but Jody would spend the day thinking about what it would have been like if she and Neal were walking through the lovely old town together, holding hands, maybe taking the ferry boat to nearby St. John and holding each other close on one of the beaches she had read about.

Terry was boyishly eager to show Jody the Virgin Islands. He took her to Flag Hill on an aerial tramway, to a crest from which they admired a breathtaking vista of blues and greens. Afterward, they joined the throngs of bargain hunters who had gotten off not only the *Caribe Queen* but several other enormous cruise ships to enjoy a shopping spree in the delightful shops of Charlotte Amalie. Allowed six hundred dollars in duty-free purchases, the passengers were happily accumulating lingerie, jewelry, fine crystal and china and even stereo equipment from all over the world.

As they strolled from shop to shop, admiring the melange of Danish, Dutch, Spanish and French buildings that lined the avenues, Jody discovered that although the prices were much lower than those found in comparable stores back home, the merchandise was geared to people who could afford vacations on cruise ships, not employees who worked on them. A pale yellow chiffon gown with flowing butterfly sleeves, probably the most beautiful dress she had ever seen, was priced far beyond Jody's means. Besides, she was not going to get paid until the ship returned to Miami. Reluctantly, she replaced it on its rack and told Terry that she thought she'd look at some accessories for a gown she already owned.

As they crossed the street to another shop, Terry said, "While you're looking, I'll run over to a little tobacco shop around the corner. I have a former patient who always asks me to get this dreadful rum-flavored pipe tobacco. Suppose we meet right in front of the store you're going to? Will fifteen minutes give you enough time?"

It was more than enough time for Jody to select a hand-screened print scarf with which to brighten her beige formal. No one would be fooled, she thought disconsolately, but then, she could hardly be expected to compete with a girl whose father encouraged her every whim; Diane went around looking as though life were one perpetual style show.

Terry joined her at the appointed time, empty-handed, saying, "They're fresh out of the rum stuff. I'll get it next time we're here. Anyway, I've had enough shopping, if you have. We'll take a taxi to Megan's Bay."

Megan's Bay, Jody learned, was one of the world's most beautiful beaches. They had not brought swimming attire, but it was restful to sit in canvas lounge chairs, looking out at the sailboats, conversing easily about pleasant subjects. It would have been a relaxing, if unexciting, time if Jody had not drawn in a sharp breath at the sight of a familiar figure. It couldn't be . . . but it was; Neal in the briefest black swim trunks, looking like a Grecian god who had been cast in bronze, jogging across the honey-colored sand at the water's edge. Jody did not have to look far to see Diane, lagging behind Neal but racing to catch up to him. Her long golden hair was tossed by the breeze, her golden body was displayed perfectly by the skimpiest white bikini imaginable. Diane was a sight that most people only see in Hollywood beach movies. Jody's heart sank.

Terry could not have helped seeing the magnificent pair, but he discreetly pretended that he hadn't. Before Neal and Diane could turn and run back to this section of the beach, the doctor said that he was "dying of thirst," and suggested that they'd had enough of the sun. Would Jody like to join him at his favorite Virgin Islands' cocktail lounge?

It hurt to know that Terry was feeling sorry for her. Had her reaction to the sight of Neal been so obvious? Jody tried hard, for the rest of their time on St. Thomas, to sound sprightly and carefree, but Terry must have seen through that act, too. After a single drink, he glanced at his watch, said he had an appointment with "his favorite hypochondriac" and hoped Jody wouldn't be too disappointed if they returned to the ship.

How had Terry known that she wanted to escape to her cabin, throw herself across the bed, and cry until there were no more tears left inside her?

She had apparently drifted off to sleep. Jody awoke to the sound of someone knocking on her door. She slipped into her robe as the caller introduced himself as the room steward. Jody opened her door to have the steward hand her a brightly beribboned dress box that he said had just been delivered from one of the shops in town. There was no card, but Jody didn't have to know who the sender was or what the box contained.

Half an hour later, standing before her mirror and delighted with the fit of the gown with the glamorous butterfly sleeves, Jody phoned Terry Allin to tell him she couldn't possibly accept such an expensive gift from him.

"You'll find something just exactly right for me some day," the doctor told her. "I'll start giving you hints, I collect old maps and I'm a nut for Danish crystal. Does the dress fit? You said it was your size, but you didn't try it on."

"I couldn't afford to try it on," Jody said. "Oh, Terry, why did you do a thing like that?"

"Because I'm going to escort you to the captain's gala. And I want the prettiest girl aboard ship to look prettier than ever."

Protests were ineffective. Jody could only thank Terry for his generosity and his perception. How had he known that she dreaded another appearance in one of her two weary dresses?

Afterward, hanging the lovely yellow chiffon carefully in her closet, Jody wished that love could be guided by good sense instead of the heart. It was sad that she could never fall in love with Terry; he was one of the kindest, most considerate people she had ever met. But love . . . love simply *happened,* it wasn't dictated by logic.

She should have been thinking about Terry when she tried on that confection of a gown once more later that night. She had never owned anything comparable, never looked better. Yet when she admired the reflection in her mirror, Jody was not thinking of the doctor. She was imagining herself walking into the dining room on the final, most festive night of this cruise. She pictured Neal Rainey's eyes admiring her. Oh, not that any woman aboard would detract from Diane's entrance in her beaded white creation, but hadn't Neal once called her beautiful? He might think so again. They might talk. She would try to think of the right things to say and maybe, just maybe. . . .

Jody replaced the soft yellow chiffon in her closet. She would be forever grateful to Terry. Meanwhile, she had a night to look forward to, a night when Neal might notice her again before he left the ship, before he walked out of her life and her dreams forever. Before she fell asleep again, her arms aching for the man she knew now that she loved, Jody even let herself think about being held in his arms once again and hearing him say that he needed her, wanted her, had to have her for his own. It was a foolish dream, probably a hopeless dream. But the yellow gown with the butterfly sleeves made it, somehow, a romantic dream that might just possibly come true.

Chapter Eleven

Ironically, it was Diane Westbrook's mother who turned the tide.

Early the next day, as the *Caribe Queen* cut a swath through the placid blue Caribbean on its way to Tortola, in the British Virgin Islands, Jody spotted Elise stretched out in a lounge chair in one of the sundecks. Elise was alone, staring out to sea, her eyes diverted from the book in her hand. She was delighted to see Jody and invited her to sit down in the deck chair beside her. "Just for a minute, dear. I know how busy you are."

Asked how things were going for her, Elise mentioned a few of her usual complaints about her husband, but she sounded more positive. "Oh, well, it's Dalton's vacation. He works so hard at home. And a few drinks and dropping a small fortune in the casino make him happy, so I'm not nagging him about it." Elise was less casual about her daughter. "Diane's so touchy from lack of sleep that you can say 'good morning' to her and have her snap at you. Oh, Jody, I know she's head over heels in love with that man. And he couldn't possibly be seriously interested in her."

"Why do you assume that he can't be serious?" Jody wanted to know. "They . . . they certainly seem to . . . have fun together."

"Fun, yes. But he's not some shallow fly-by-night. The man's serious about life, about his work, his values. Diane's an impetuous child. Not someone he'd want to introduce to his professional friends." Elise's index finger tapped the book. "You develop an admiration for the man when you read this."

Love and admiration were two different things, Jody thought. She refused to let anyone know that she loved Neal. And she wanted to get across the fact that she had broken up with him because he was less than admirable in her eyes. "My impression from the book was that he's terribly fond of himself. I hated that bit where he made himself sound like a knight in shining armor, up against insurmountable odds. And then, of course, at the trial. . . ."

Elise frowned uncomprehendingly. "What trial was that?"

"Oh, where that young man was accused of murder and there were all those heart-tugging references to his poor mother. It read like a television script, where you know the hero is going to triumph in the end, but first . . . " Jody was almost beginning to convince herself that she had been justified in criticizing Neal. "I couldn't read the whole chapter, but I can imagine the scene where the boy's mother throws her arms around the clever attorney and thanks him for saving her innocent son's life."

"He didn't," Elise said flatly.

"Didn't what?"

"Get him acquitted. Mr. Rainey lost that case."

Jody stared at her, shocked. "He . . . lost the case?"

"Mr. Rainey got his client off with a life sentence, but his client was guilty. He flew into a violent rage one day, called his lawyer every name under the sun and admitted that he'd killed that poor man. It was agonizing for Mr. Rainey. Here he'd been thinking of himself as some sort of savior, but he learned how little he knew about people, how your judgment gets all clouded when you start to think of yourself in heroic terms. The end of that chapter made me cry, Jody. The man was made to look like a fool before all his professional friends. He was seen on television, in the courtroom hallway, with the client's mother screaming at him. And. in his book he writes about learning a lesson in humility."

"Humility?" Jody sounded dubious.

"Yes, humility. He hoped that mistake, that failure, would make him a more discriminating judge of character. But, more than that, he hoped that the experience would make him a better *person*. Diane couldn't begin to understand a man like that. And he couldn't possibly take a serious interest in her."

A sickening feeling gnawed at Jody's conscience. She had skimmed a few pages and made a judgment—a prejudiced, inaccurate judgment. No wonder Neal had turned away from her! "I . . . didn't read the book very carefully," she admitted.

"I'm almost finished with it," Elise said. "I wish Diane would read it, too, but she's only interested in showing her friends back home the picture on the back cover. And there's no telling her that there's a lot more to Mr. Rainey than his handsome face."

Jody was kept busy helping Prez until the dinner hour. Then, deciding she wasn't hungry, Jody settled herself in her bed and stayed awake until she had read Neal's book from cover to cover.

She had never read a more honest confession of failures and weaknesses, never felt that she was in the presence of a strong man, sincerely trying to improve himself by facing his flaws directly and openly.

It was nearly midnight when she closed the book. Would Terry be at the midnight buffet? He usually was, and she needed his advice, even though, he, too, had misjudged Neal, though maybe he had done so out of a personal jealousy.

Jody dressed hurriedly and took the elevator to the Golden Grotto, where the "movable feast" was being served tonight. She found Terry carrying his plate to a secluded corner table. When she had helped herself to small portions of everything from the lavish buffet, Jody joined the doctor and came right to the point. "I said terrible things to Neal and I was wrong. I owe him an apology, Terry, but . . . I don't have the nerve to walk right up to him and say I'm sorry. I'd die if I got . . . you know. An icy rejection. What can I do? I was so unjust!"

The doctor's round blue eyes held Jody's for a moment as he said, "You really do, don't you. You really do love the man."

It was too late for denials. Jody nodded her head miserably, tears springing up in her eyes.

Terry speared a forkful of *Fricatelles de Veau Niçoise*, holding it in midair as he said, "Gift shop's closed at this hour, so you can't buy one of those sorry-about-that cards. But you can talk to the bartender and have a bottle of nice, unpretentious wine sent to Rainey's suite. Write a note on a cocktail napkin. And then wait for a phone call."

"What if he's with someone else?" Jody worried aloud. "Or what if he reads the note and . . . just goes back to sleep? I'd be so humiliated . . ."

"Notes written on cocktail napkins are always taken very seriously," Terry joked. He nodded at Jody's plate. "Finish your supper and get out of here. I charge double for my advice after twelve thirty."

Shortly afterward, Jody thanked him. Terry gave her hand an encouraging squeeze and she hurried to the bar to order the "nice, unpretentious wine."

No more than ten minutes later, Jody was back in her cabin. Suddenly, a ringing telephone became the most important sound in the world. If he was in his suite, Neal would have read her note by now. But he might be in one of the lounges. He might be dancing with Diane. He might be asleep, finding the note and the wine an unwanted interruption. What if he *never* called?

He did. The jangling sound she had been hoping for

146

startled Jody, nevertheless. She picked up the receiver, trying not to sound too breathless. "Hello?"

"I have a problem," Neal's deep, resonant voice said. "A lovely lady just surprised me with a touching note and a bottle of excellent French wine."

Jody's heart refused to stop pounding, but she assumed Neal's light-hearted sound. "Is that a problem?"

"Only if there's no one to share it with. If you don't mind drinking out of water glasses, I'm wide awake and I'm decent. Could you come up and . . . talk to me?"

"At this hour?" Jody was sure he could hear the hammering of her heart; it seemed clearly audible in the cabin.

"Seize the moment, as they say. I'd come to see you, but I suspect this place is roomier."

Shortly afterward, her beige gown perked up with the newly purchased scarf, her makeup fresh and her hair brushed with a none-too-steady hand, Jody was ready. Except for her innocent visit with Terry Allin, she had never before spent time with a man in his room. Jody felt uneasy, yet she knew that if she had refused, Neal might never have called her again. She left her cabin with a mingled anticipation and dread.

The upper decks were almost deserted, the air balmy and caressing. Jody felt on the verge of something momentous, something that might change her life forever.

Neal met her at his door, a maroon silk dressing gown over his pajamas. He smiled broadly, admiring Jody's long dress and saying, "If I had known this was going to be a formal affair, I'd have worn something less comfortable." As Neal ushered Jody into his suite, which was identical with that occupied by the Westbrooks except for changes in color and fabrics, Neal complimented Jody on her "beautiful new dress."

"I've worn this over and over," Jody said. "I'm sure you've seen it many times before."

"I don't particularly notice clothing." Neal gestured at one of the two long sofas in the room and Jody sat down. Her gift bottle of wine rested on the cocktail table, flanked by two of the tall water glasses that were standard equipment in all the ship's rooms. Dropping down to sit beside Jody, Neal added, "I'm always too busy looking at faces to notice dresses. Looking into eyes. Much more interested in the gift than the wrappings."

Jody thought of two dresses that were hanging in shipboard closets, both intended to impress Neal. No, the white beaded fantasy that Diane would wear was still to be delivered, but the yellow chiffon with the butterfly sleeves, ironically a gift from another man, was going to be worn especially for Neal.

"Shall we?" Neal opened the wine bottle and poured a splash into each of the two glasses. He didn't propose a toast. Instead he asked, "Do you know how happy I was to get your note? I've been going around thinking that maybe you were right, that day on the beach. Plunging into manic activity, maybe trying to prove something to myself."

"You aren't going to convince me that you're insecure," Jody told him.

"I was having a great time with you, Jody, and then we had that disagreement. . . ." He took Jody's glass out of her hand. "Anyway I'm glad you changed your mind about me. There's so little time left. Next week I'll be back in the real world. I want to remember this time. I want to remember being with you."

Their glasses sat on the table. And Neal had reached out for Jody. She slipped into his arms easily, almost hungrily, not quite sure that what was happening was real. Their first kiss was long and lingering. Neal kissed her again with a growing ardor. His hands ran across her cheeks, her throat, trembling and warm. She felt him fumbling with the knot in her scarf, then untying it and letting it fall to the sofa. "This is beautiful," he said in a throaty whisper. "This is right, Jody. We don't have to be afraid of each other. This is so right!"

It seemed that they could not get close enough to each other, Jody's senses swimming in a heated sea of passions she had never before known to exist inside her. His hands explored her body, his breath quickening, kisses raining down on her face, her neck, her covered breasts. I won't be sorry afterward, Jody told herself silently. I love him. I'm the luckiest woman in the world.

The shrill sound was a blasphemy, an obscenity that shattered the mood. "At this hour?" Neal extracted himself from their tight embrace. "It must be after two."

The telephone rang again before he crossed over to the desk to pick up the receiver. He sounded surly, almost snarling his, "Yes?"

Jody touched at her tousled hair, smoothing down her long dress. Neal was listening to someone on the phone, his handsome face twisted into an annoyed scowl. After a long wait, Jody heard him say, "Yes, I know it's a great band. I've heard them. I'm just not into disco tonight. No, I'm not too tired. I'm . . . busy. I have a visitor."

Jody wondered about the reaction on the other end of the line. Whoever was calling (and she almost knew) would know that he wasn't having a conference with legal colleagues at this time of the morning. She heard Neal saying, "No, I'm afraid not. No way." And after another long pause, Neal said, "I don't know about tomorrow. I may take a tour with some of the attorneys from California. I've spent very little time with them and the cruise is almost over. Yes, sure. Yes, if it works

149

out that way, I'll be in touch. Enjoy yourself and don't forget that tomorrow is another day."

Neal had never mentioned her name, but there could be no doubt that he had been talking with Diane Westbrook. His face looked a little flushed as he acknowledged his caller's identity. "Crazy, wild kid. Wants me to come to the Castaways Club. I'm no longer in my teens. I felt like telling Diane that I barely made it through dinner tonight."

Neal smiled and returned to his place on the sofa. "What a rotten piece of timing." He started to take Jody back into his arms, but she drew away from him. "Something wrong, Jody?"

"I feel that I'm disrupting your evening," she said.

"My evening was spent with a good book," Neal protested. "Peaceful but dull, until the steward rapped on my door. Jody, you can't know how happy I was to hear from you, how wonderful it is to have you here with me."

Somehow, for Jody, the call had completely destroyed the rapport that had been so overwhelming a few minutes earlier. It was as though Diane was in the room. How many times *had* she been in this room? Neal had spent most of his waking hours with Diane during the past week. At the moment, she was probably furious, feeling the sting of rejection. Neal didn't have to tell her that he had a "visitor." Was that part of his game, encouraging women, making them jealous with others, *using* them?

She felt cheapened, suddenly. Maybe she had been wrong about Neal's conceit and his general attitude toward other people—toward himself. But he could not deny that he had encouraged the interest of a nineteen-year-old male collector.

Jody got to her feet.

"You're not leaving?" Neal said.

"It's late," Jody said. "I'm not a teen-ager anymore,

either." She tried to sound casual, to not close the door between them. Tomorrow she might feel differently.

Neal rose and walked her to the door. "I'm sorry I was so obvious. I really meant to sit here and just talk with you. You don't make that easy, Jody. You're so lovely and so . . . so real. If I came on too strong, you'll have to share a little of the blame."

Jody nodded. She could not deny that she had wanted Neal as much, perhaps more, than he had wanted her.

"We'll talk tomorrow," he said. If his feelings were hurt, he was being clever at hiding them. "I hear Tortola's a fantastic place. And we'll have two days there. Suppose I talk to the purser about renting a skiff and getting around to some of the smaller islands? I was reading tonight about Virgin Gorda and the natural pools they call The Baths. We could have lunch at a place I read about, called The Bitter End Yacht Club. Does that sound like a good day to you?"

Jody had to admit that it sounded wonderful. But she couldn't resist asking, "Are you sure you don't have other plans? I'm sure Diane must be counting on you to show her around."

Neal frowned. And then his perfect face broadened in a wide smile. "Do I detect a note of jealousy?" He clasped Jody in his arms, pressing her close in an ecstatic bear hug. "If I thought for a minute you were making noises like a . . . a jealous woman, I'd be delirious."

How could he make fun of having the power to make women jealous? "I was just trying to be fair," Jody said in the iciest tone she could muster. "After all, you *have* given Diane the idea that . . ."

"The idea that I feel terribly sorry for her," Neal said soberly.

"Sorry for her?"

"Certainly. Her *nouveau riche* father is unbelievably coarse. Imagine a bright young girl being cooped up in a suite with her parents for all this time? Any young woman her age would be miserable."

"I hadn't noticed that she spends too much time 'cooped up' with her parents," Jody reminded Neal.

"Well, all right, I've been helping her to stay busy. She plays great tennis and she can be very amusing. I'm on vacation and I get tired of . . . courtroom shop-talk." Neal lowered his voice. "When you decided that I wasn't the sort of person you want to know, I . . . I just turned elsewhere for my . . . casual companion-ship."

"I'm not sure Diane thinks of it as all that casual," Jody said.

Neal looked astounded. "She couldn't think other-wise! I made it absolutely clear that it couldn't be anything else." He scowled. "You're still making a cad out of me, Jody. I was fair with her. I said the same things to her that . . ."

"That you said to me." Jody nodded toward the sofa with a meaningful look. "And here I am."

Neal dismissed the implication with laughter. Then, folding Jody in his arms he said, "You're not comparing yourself with a crazy, mixed-up kid, are you? Jody, if anyone else had stood me off twice in a row, the way you've done, I'd be furious. Do you know why I'm not? Oh, I'm disappointed. I want you so much that it hurts. But . . . I can't think of you as one of those . . . those shipboard flings people talk about. I want to know you better. I want to know you for a long, long time." Neal's head bent down and Jody found herself respond-ing to another of his sense-inflaming kisses.

For a moment, after Neal had released her lips, Jody thought of telling him she had changed her mind. But instinct told her it was better to leave now. She was too confused to make important decisions. One minute she worshiped the man, the next she distrusted him, doubting his sincerity. Thoroughly bewildered, Jody knew only that, for better or for worse, she did love him. And no amount of analyzing would remove the heat of kisses that burned on her lips long after they had parted.

Chapter Twelve

Jody's first glimpse of Tortola, the next morning, was an experience she would never forget. From the turquoise waters and sparkling white sands, the island rose to a height of a thousand feet, its soaring volcano covered with lush forests, its shoreline edged with swaying palms and flowering shrubs. Pristine yachts dotted the harbor, looking like toy boats compared with the *Caribe Queen*. It was a sight out of Jody's most wishful dreams. And the thought that she might get to explore this paradise with Neal made it doubly exciting. He had said something about a meeting with his colleagues in the morning; they had not made a date. But now that Jody was in Neal's good graces again, she was hopeful.

Her joyous mood was short-lived. When the elevator stopped on the deck occupied by Neal and the Westbrooks, only one passenger got on. It was Diane, looking tense and weary, though still beautiful in a clinging blue and white floral pantsuit. She looked changed, somehow. Her eyes, more heavily made up than usual, looked washed out, and there were hard little lines around her pretty pink-lustered mouth. Jody's "good morning" was acknowledged with a cool nod.

There were several seconds before the elevator started its rise to the Nautilus deck. To fill the uncomfortable silence, Jody said, "Isn't Tortola beautiful? I can't wait to see it, can you?"

She was rewarded with a baleful stare.

Jody's second attempt at being friendly brought forth an even more chilling response. She mentioned the Captain's Gala, scheduled for the next night. "Your dad tells me you've gotten an absolutely fabulous dress for the occasion."

"He probably told you the price, too," Diane said. There was a sneering contempt in her voice as she said the new gown was "about as decent as anything you can find outside of Paris." And she apparently couldn't resist a dig at Jody. "If you wear that little beige number again, what about black accessories? My mother has some to go with one of her dresses, but she'll be wearing something new. It's just a thought."

Jody thanked her for the fashion advice. When they reached the Aquamarine deck, she waited for Diane to get off the elevator. "Coming to breakfast?"

Diane made a dismissing motion with her perfectly manicured hands. "I'm meeting someone on the sundeck."

Jody wished her a fun day on Tortola and stepped out of the elevator. She caught an even more startling view of the island from the stern of the Aquamarine deck. Pausing for a long look at the tropical wonder before her, Jody was joined by Terry Allin. He was delighted with Jody's reaction to the island.

"You have to get close up to really appreciate it," the doctor said. "It's like one big bouquet of hibiscus and frangipani and bougainvillea. I never get over the thrill of seeing flamboyant trees in bloom, those enormous orange clusters of flowers against dark green leaves." He leaned against the rail. "I suppose you have plans for the day?"

"Only tentative," Jody said.

"But your note and the wine did the job? You're back in Rainey's good graces?"

Jody thanked him for his suggestion and told him about her visit to Neal's suite, assuring him that her stay was brief and "uneventful." "We didn't want to

155

stay up too late and miss any of this." Jody nodded toward the tower of greenery.

"I hope he got up in time for it," Terry said. "Though I think you should know that you weren't the last visitor to Neal Rainey's suite last night."

"I'm sure I must have been," Jody told him. "It was past two in the morning when I left."

"And it was just past three when I was called out of bed by Elise Westbrook. I thought she may have been faking something again, but I was wrong. She had a genuine headache and nothing to take for it. I gave her a strong analgesic and talked with her for a while. Her husband was still up at the all-night bar when I came into their suite. He arrived while I was there. And after I'd left the two of them, who did I run into but their daughter?"

"Coming back from the disco," Jody guessed.

"She wasn't coming back to the suite. And if she'd been dancing in that diaphanous white thing that looked like a negligee, she may have caused a few nervous breakdowns. But she must have had an appointment. She was knocking on your attorney friend's door."

"I heard Neal talk to her on the phone. He didn't tell me . . ."

"Of course he wouldn't have told you he was expecting her," Terry said irritably. "But you know she wouldn't have been knocking on his door at that hour if he wasn't. I was discreet. Got out of there in a hurry. Not even sure that Diane noticed me."

Jody felt a stab of resentment. Why had Terry told her this story, taking the glow off of her happy reconciliation with Neal? For a moment her resentment was directed at Terry, and then she realized that it was Neal who deserved her ire. Was he the person Diane was meeting on the sundeck this morning? If so, he might be skipping his breakfast meeting with the other attorneys this morning. They would probably be touring

Tortola with each other. Neal had been less than honest with her, Jody thought. She would never give him a chance to hurt her again or rake her with the jealousy that was tearing her apart now.

"I hope my bit of gossip didn't upset you," Terry was saying. "I was trying to be very unselfish last night, hoping everything would work out well for you, Jody."

"It was all right," Jody said airily. "Frankly, I was . . . a little disturbed because I don't like to have bad feelings between myself and the other passengers. We . . . buried the hatchet."

Terry was seeing right through her pretense. "And you're still friends. Good." He didn't remind Jody that she had admitted, the night before, that she was in love with Neal.

Still pretending that what Neal did and did not do was of no importance to her, Jody said, "If you're going ashore, Doctor, and you don't have other plans, would you mind my tagging along today?"

Terry was surprised and delighted. "Wonderful. You'll get to pick your first mango and we'll swim in *pina coladas.*" There was an adoring expression on Terry's face, a gentleness that Jody had seen more and more often in recent days. Once again, she wished that she could see Terry as more than just a friend.

And Terry was not merely a friend to her; he was thoughtful of others, too. At the breakfast table that morning, he showed genuine interest in the excited chatter of the ladies from California. Three crew members had agreed to escort them around Tortola, an arrangement that Jody was certain had been made by the doctor.

Jody talked briefly with the student who collected butterflies, learning that he planned to hike up Tortola's forest-covered hills in search of a rare moth indigenous to the island. When that conversation lapsed, Jody's attention was drawn to that of the Westbrooks, at the end of the table.

There were meals during which Elise and Dalton barely exchanged a word between them. This morning was different. They seemed to be ignoring the others and their dialog seemed to be rising in fervor as well as volume. If they were aware that their conversation might be heard by others at the table, they didn't seem to care. They didn't even stop when one of the crew members came to tell Dr. Allin that he was wanted in his office immediately.

With Terry gone and the student busy demolishing an enormous breakfast, Jody was no longer distracted. She couldn't help overhearing what the Westbrooks were saying.

Elise was adamant. "You didn't say one word to her, Dalton! You acted as though she should get a pat on the back for good behavior!"

"What did you want me to do?" her husband fumed. "Put Diane on bread and water for the rest of this trip? I . . . I felt sorry for the kid. He had no right to embarrass her that way."

"I think he had every right," Elise said, lowering her voice. "She could have placed *him* in a compromising position. And what about us, Dalton? Didn't you want to die of shame when Mr. Rainey came storming into our suite in the middle of the night, dragging Diane by the arm and giving us a lecture about . . . about giving some proper attention to our 'spoiled brat daughter'? I felt so terrible!"

"How do you think Diane felt?" Dalton asked. But he sounded less sure of himself than usual.

"She brought it on herself," Elise insisted. "Imagine knocking on that man's door at that hour, offering herself to him. He was sound asleep, he said. And he didn't have any interest in Diane except to play tennis with her and do a little sightseeing. He *said* that, Dalton, and I believe the man. Instead of being furious with him, you ought to have a long talk with Diane. Right after we've had breakfast!"

Jody gulped down the rest of her coffee and excused herself. She could understand Diane's icy attitude now. And she could only be grateful that she had not made another scene with Neal, only to be proven wrong once again. Why was she willing to believe the worst about him? Was it because she thought Neal was too good to be true?

Jody headed for her cabin to freshen up. She was miserable because she had believed Terry's gossip. Not that it had been told to her with some vindictive motive in mind; Terry had misunderstood the situation. She couldn't blame Terry, but Jody could blame herself for having so little faith in Neal. Hadn't he told her that he had nothing but a friendly, almost paternal interest in Diane? Worst of all, Jody was now going to spend a day with a man she liked and respected instead of with the man she loved. Now, even if Neal decided to ask her to tour their last port of call before San Juan with him she would have to give her regrets.

There was a note on Jody's dressing table when she stepped into her cabin. Before she could open the envelope, the telephone rang. It was Terry's nurse, reporting that the doctor was going to be busy all morning. He was sorry, but one of the kitchen helpers had suffered an accident. He hoped that Jody would have time to join one of the guided shore excursions.

Seconds after she dropped the receiver, Jody was reading a note in Neal's now familiar handwriting:

Dear Jody,
Tied up with a breakfast meeting until ten. Hope
you can wait that long and meet me in the library.
I'm looking forward to a wonderful day and hope
you are, too.

N.

Jody was sure that her delighted yelp was heard in the cabins across the hall. She read the note twice, then gathered up her coral-colored bikini, a huge beach towel, suntan lotion, and a light shawl for evening. She stuffed everything into the straw bag Neal had bought for her during that fabulous day in Curaçao. Dressed in a pale blue terry-cloth ensemble, she arrived at Prez's office minutes afterward, enormously relieved to learn that, except for helping him supervise an orderly disembarkation for the shore-going passengers, her day would be free to get acquainted with Tortola.

Several times during that day, Jody thought that if she was in the habit of keeping a diary, this day would be recorded as "perfect." After a hand-holding tour of Road Town, Tortola's charming capital, Jody and Neal boarded a small chartered boat at the Village Cay Marina. They visited tiny Cooper Island and sailed, via the scenic Sir Francis Drake Channel, to beautiful Gorda Island, where enormous boulders edged the crystalline waters of fresh, natural pools.

They swam in one of the blue-green pools, laughing and splashing each other like children, delighted to be in each other's company. And when Neal reached out his hand to pull Jody out of the water, he drew her directly into his embrace. Their lips met easily and naturally now, but there was no less ardor in their kisses. Pressed against Neal's bare chest, feeling the rain of kisses with which he covered her face, her throat, then her lips again, Jody thought of how close she had come to losing this exciting man and she clung to his neck like someone drowning, one hand pressing his head closer to her own.

As Neal's hands roamed over her body, setting every nerve and muscle on fire, Jody was overwhelmed by her own passionate response to Neal's touch. How strong he was, yet how tender, as he bent to kiss her almost bared breasts, his fingers caressing her back, dropping down to explore every curve of her body. Yes, and how thrilling it was to hear his breathless murmuring as he became aware of the unquenchable thirst for love he had aroused in her: "Jody, oh, Jody, why did it take me so long to find you, darling?"

She yearned to hear Neal say that he loved her. It was too soon for that, Jody knew. Yet in every look, every word, every kiss, every caress of his hands, wasn't he telling her what she wanted to hear? Was this really love; a mutually shared love? It had to be! It seemed that this enchanted never-never land of crystal waters and tumbling cascades of brilliant flowers had been created for them alone.

Later, as they walked through this tropical paradise with their fingers entwined, there were long periods of silence when their only communication came through the pressure of Neal's hands. Awed by the loveliness of their flower-bedecked surroundings, they were quiet at times, but always there was the rapport that told Jody that this was where they belonged—together.

But between those silent, rapturous moments of togetherness, there was joyous laughter, too, even when Jody learned to her dismay that one didn't pick bananas from their stalks unless one was wearing old, expendable clothes. Her blue terry cloth top was stained by orange-brown blotches. "And from what I read somewhere, banana stains are an indelible dye," Neal said. "No getting it out. I'm so sorry, Jody. You look so lovely in that outfit."

"I'll have to go back to the ship and change," Jody said, surveying the damage.

"No, you won't," Neal argued. "If your shawl won't cover the stains, we'll find something for you to wear in one of the shops. And you'll be the loveliest lady I ever took to dinner, no matter what you wear."

Although they took pains to avoid the more heavily trafficked tourist spots, it was impossible to avoid running into other passengers from the *Caribe Queen*. One of the larger escorted tour groups occupied most of the seafood restaurant they chose for their dinner.

Neal was the first to notice that the Westbrook family was among those present. Dalton was taking pictures of everyone in the party. Elise, matronly and sedate in a simple hunter green pantsuit, was sipping a non-alcoholic fruit drink that was a specialty of the house, looking subdued. Diane, pouting and sullen, sat beside her mother and toyed with her dinner without speaking to anyone. She was smartly dressed, as always, but she looked somewhat bedraggled in spite of it. She not only didn't stare in Neal's direction; she seemed to be avoiding eye contact with him.

Jody actually felt sorry for the girl. Furthermore, her respect for Neal rose when she stopped to think that he had not said one word to her, and probably not a word to anyone else, about the incident with his uninvited, early-morning visitor. If gossip about Diane's behavior had gotten around the ship, it hadn't been started by Neal Rainey.

Jody was happily exhausted when Neal saw her back to the *Caribe Queen*. They had shared a long, idyllic day and neither Jody nor Neal were in the mood for dancing or partying. But they were reluctant to go their separate ways. For a long time Neal stood at the rail on the Aquamarine deck with his arm around Jody's waist.

It was a caressingly warm night, the air perfumed by the flowers of Tortola as a breeze blew over that lovely island and out to sea. Stars had never shone more brightly. Their reflections turned the Caribbean into a velvet carpet that someone had dusted with diamonds. Once again, Neal and Jody were silenced by awesome beauty. Was Neal thinking, as Jody was, that tomorrow night they would be back in San Juan, and that from there the ship would be returning to Miami? This cruise would be over and Neal would be going back home. Would Jody ever see him again? Or was this another experience that would end, as that other summer romance had ended, when the vacation was over?

Oh, but there was no comparison between that

callow "first love" and what Jody felt now with Neal's grip tightening around her waist. Yet a tremulous feeling of imminent loss shuddered through her. For in spite of Neal's affectionate attention, in spite of the emotion that poured from him like molten lava when Neal held her in his arms, Jody had to remember that he had never retracted that initial warning that he was not interested in a serious relationship with any woman. Nor had he spoken the words that Jody yearned to hear.

Maybe it was just physical tiredness that brought on her melancholy feeling. She felt close to tears when Neal saw her to her door and kissed her good night. Tiredness? Or the knowledge that she loved Neal with every fiber of her being and that these beautiful moments they had shared together might soon be nothing more than a memory? He kissed her with a poignant tenderness that made Jody wonder if the same thoughts had crept into Neal's mind. It was a long, long kiss, not unlike the kind exchanged by lovers at train stations and airports, when both are touched and subdued by the realization that they will never again know a day or a night like this one, and that this is the time of parting.

Chapter Thirteen

It was just as well that Jody did not see Neal in the dining room at breakfast. If he had invited her to go ashore with him, to see what they had missed of San Juan on their first stop, Jody would have had to beg off; Prez was in a frenzied state when Jody reported to his office at nine.

Prez's words were addressed to Jody, but as he paced the floor of the small room, he sounded as though he were having an agitated conversation with himself. It seemed that the stewards who were to have decorated the public rooms for the captain's gala had "failed him." One of the young men had stepped on a sea urchin spine and now, pumped full of antibiotics by Dr. Allin, was indisposed. The other had managed to injure himself in a minor sailing accident at Virgin Gorda. Prez took it all as a personal affront. "Now I'm stuck with explaining my Total Environment Lighted Caribbean Garden Concept to someone else," he complained. "That leaves you, dear girl, to get the decorations together, talk to the electrician about my special lighting, and see that my Friends Forever idea is implemented."

Prez had dreamed up an elaborate ceremony for the customary exchange of addresses with which most of the passengers ended their cruise. It was usually done, he told Jody, during their last night at sea. But many of the attorneys would be flying home from Puerto Rico instead of sailing on to Miami. "So we're under pressure," Prez said.

He was telling Jody, in essence, that she would probably not be setting foot on dry land today; Neal would have to drive to the fabled Puerto Rican rain forest without her. She was disappointed, of course. The thought of not spending this last day ashore with Neal ached like something hard and unswallowable stuck in her throat. But she wasn't on board to enjoy a vacation. She was an employee, and one with much to learn.

Jody stayed busy until noon, wondering from time to time where Neal was, if he had attempted to contact her, what he was doing, who he had chosen to keep him company. The jobs that Prez had made to seem insurmountably complicated were easily disposed of by lunchtime. Jody checked back at her cabin several times to see if there were any written messages from Neal. Each time, she returned to the office feeling heavy with disappointment.

By early afternoon, Prez's "friendship forever" ritual was well organized. The Aquamarine dining room had, magically, become a tropical flower garden. Jody returned to her cabin, looking forward to a long, leisurely time in which to prepare herself for the exciting evening ahead.

There *was* a note on her dressing table! Jody opened the small envelope hurriedly, breathless with anticipation. Then her spirits sank. The message, scribbled in an unfamiliar hand and hard to read, said:

> Jody,
> *Have a little something for you. Can you stop by our suite for a minute? Haven't been able to reach you by phone.*

Jody had to squint to make out the signature. The note was signed by Elise Westbrook.

It was a well-meant "little something" that waited for Jody in the Westbrooks' luxurious suite. But it was also a humiliating gift, especially since it had been Diane's idea.

"I've been telling my family how very kind you've been to me," Elise said as she presented Jody with an elaborately wrapped gift box. "Diane and I were in the gift shop this morning—I've been keeping very close tabs on her. And, anyway, Diane thought this would be a way to show my appreciation."

Jody opened the box to find a shimmering gold-sequined bolero jacket.

"I hope you like it," Elise said, beaming. "Diane thought it would be just perfect tonight with your . . ."

"With my old beige dress." Jody hadn't meant her comment to sound so cryptic.

"Oh, it's a lovely dress," Elise said. She apparently didn't know that her daughter had chosen this way of sneering at Jody's comparatively meager wardrobe.

Jody had no alternative but to offer profuse thanks for the shimmering jacket, though she had no intention of wearing it that night. She was replacing the gift in its box when Diane charged into the suite, barely nodding at Jody and complaining about the "idiots in that madhouse of a beauty salon" who couldn't understand that she didn't want her hair "all backcombed and sprayed stiff and phony-looking."

Jody was forced to thank Diane, too, for the sequined bolero.

"Glad you like it," Diane said, smiling. Somehow her smile was as beguiling as a knife thrust. "We all want to look stunning tonight."

"I think Jody always looks nice," Elise said. To prove her admiration of Jody's good taste, she gestured at the straw bag Jody had set down on the cocktail table. "I wish I'd bought some of those for gifts. Where did you buy it, dear?"

"Neal Rainey got that for me the day we spent on Curaçao. The vendor was so funny! He thought we were honeymooners and I was so embarrassed!" Jody could have kicked herself for her thoughtlessness.

Diane's expression froze. "Really." She changed the subject abruptly from Jody's good taste to her own. "You must see what I picked out for Mother in this quaint little boutique in Charlotte Amalie. Show her what you're wearing tonight, Mother."

Elise protested, but her daughter insisted. Sliding open the oversized closet, Elise took out a gray brocade gown, simply cut, the rich fabric shot with gold threads. "The fabric's from China," she said as Jody admired the dress. "I thought it was a little plain. . . . Diane accuses me of wearing 'showgirl costumes' most of the time. But . . . do you think it would be too flashy if I wore my favorite brooch with it?"

Wanting Jody's opinion as well as Diane's, Elise unlocked a dresser drawer and then a metal jewelry case. She held the flower-shaped emerald and gold pin against her shoulder and then against the V-neckline of her gown. "What do you think? Or shouldn't I wear it at all?"

"It's such an unfussy bodice," Jody said, "I think you should wear it. At the neckline, I'd say."

Jody was starting to leave when Dalton came in from the bedroom, yawning, his eyes bleary from sleep. It was necessary to repeat her thanks for the third time, and Jody was forced to listen to Dalton's expansive bragging. "Nothing but the best for the help, I always say. You've been real good to the wife, honey. I told her, buy that little girl somethin' nice and don't bother looking at the price tag." He seemed unaware of the embarrassment he created in his wife, his daughter, or in Jody.

They talked for a moment about what a big evening tonight was going to be, and how much everyone aboard wished that the cruise could go on indefinitely. Jody reminded them that there would only be an afternoon's pause before she would be at sea again.

"Yes, but the passengers won't be the same," Diane said pointedly. "You probably won't see any of the people aboard . . . ever again."

For a moment, Diane's eyes locked with Jody's. It was a chilling experience that left Jody shaken. Why did I mention the day with Neal on Curaçao? Jody wondered. Bad enough that Neal isn't spending any time with Diane anymore and that her mother has finally gotten up the strength to draw in the reins. Diane must be fuming inside, feeling humiliated enough without having Jody remind her that she's been "replaced" in Neal's affections. Outwardly, Diane was being untypically pleasant, almost too pleasant. But in her eyes Jody saw a hateful venom that disturbed her for a long time after she had left the Westbrooks' suite.

Jody's spirits brightened when she closed her cabin door behind her. She was anxious to do something different with her hair. The yellow chiffon gown should be hung inside the bathroom while she showered; one of the sleeves was creased and irons were not permitted in the cabins. Not that any of the passengers, except the ladies from California, would ever deign to press their own clothes. In spite of the fact that she hadn't heard from Neal, Jody was excited about the evening that lay ahead. Even though Neal would not be escorting her, he would be there. Maybe he was still on shore and would call her when he came back to the ship. Maybe. . . .

Jody's thoughts were a happy jumble as she took her precious dress from the closet and hung it inside the bathroom door. She took her time in the shower, was painstaking with the arrangement of her hair, and, finally, satisfied with her makeup, slipped into the yellow dress.

Before the full-length door mirror, Jody lifted her arms to see the full effect of the winglike sleeves. She had never before owned anything as beautiful, never before been as happy with her own reflection. She would never be able to thank Terry enough. And how grateful she was that he understood; they would never be more than friends, but what good friends they would always be!

Someone knocked on the door. It had to be the room steward, Jody guessed. Maybe a note from Neal. It *had* to be a note from Neal. Maybe he had tried to call her while she was with the Westbrooks, or in the shower. . . .

Jody opened the door and gasped. It *was* the room steward. But he was accompanied by two other men, one of whom she recognized as the ship's security guard. The other man, resplendent in his white and gold uniform, was Captain Di Marro!

It was the beginning of a nightmare. The captain, who was invariably pleasant and poised, seemed grim and uncomfortable. "I hope you will understand, Miss Sommers, that our presence in no way implies that you are under any suspicion. But we have a responsibility to our passengers, and we want our crew to be totally absolved before we continue our investigation."

"Investigation of *what?*" Jody asked.

Nightmare! It was the security guard who explained that a valuable piece of jewelry was missing from one of the passenger suites. It was insured, of course. For close to eighteen thousand dollars. And the insurance company would expect a thorough search of the ship. Especially the quarters of the only person, outside the immediate family, who had been in the Westbrooks' suite when the brooch was last seen.

Jody was stunned. "She . . . Mrs. Westbrook can't find her emerald brooch? It was sitting on the cocktail table when I left their suite."

"With your permission," the security officer said. He and the steward began a methodical search of the cabin.

Jody stood horrified as they turned the sofa bed mattresses, opened drawers, riffled through the few items that still remained in her suitcases. They were checking her makeup case when the captain said, "This is most unfortunate, Miss Sommers. I hope you understand."

"Of course," Jody said. "It's a beautiful pin."

"You told me you did see it?" The captain looked distressed.

"Oh, yes. Mrs. Westbrook has worn it to dinner a few times. And she was asking me today whether to wear it on her shoulder or . . ." Jody stopped short, unable to believe that the men were going through her closet, fishing in pockets, pressing their hands along the length of clothing as if looking for a telltale lump. "Elise knows I'd never take anything that didn't belong to me!"

"Mrs. Westbrook hasn't accused you," Captain Di Marro said. Then in a quiet voice he added, "You see, we have had passengers report missing valuables. And then they remember, when their heads are a bit clearer, that they'd hidden the missing item in some strange place. I'm sure that we have the same situation here. And I'm so sorry for this interruption." He surveyed Jody with a fatherly smile. "Had I known what a decorative asset you would be this evening, I would have insisted that you be seated at my table."

Jody thanked him. And then her eyes widened in shock. The room steward had taken her straw bag from the bedside chair. Reaching inside, he had removed Jody's extra key, her address book, her compact and spare lipstick, a few shells that she had found on the beach the day before, a worn leather wallet. And finally, looking shocked himself, he held in his hand a sparkling floral design in glittering green and gold.

170

There was total silence in the room, except for Jody's heavy breathing. "How did that get there?" she said when the accusing silence became unbearable. "I didn't put it there! I'll swear the pin was sitting on the glass table when I left."

They were more embarrassed than Jody. The brooch was handed over to the captain without a word from the man who had found it.

"I'm not a thief!" Jody protested. "If I had wanted to steal something, I would have hidden it somewhere. You've got to know that . . . I didn't . . . !"

Three pairs of eyes were burning into her face. She was protesting too much. Indignant, stunned, outraged, she was protesting too much. And they didn't believe her. She knew from their stoic expressions that they didn't believe her!

She was still not being formally accused of theft. The captain simply said, "Circumstantial evidence, Miss Sommers. I have no choice but to report it to the gentleman who made the complaint—Mr. Westbrook. And you have my promise that we will continue our investigation."

"I can swear that somebody put that pin into my purse," Jody cried. "I can tell you who did it and why!"

The captain held up a restraining hand. "If the Westbrooks press charges, we'll want a full statement from you, Miss Sommers."

"I want to make it now!" Jody cried. "You're . . . you're making a thief out of me without any chance to face my accusers! Diane Westbrook hates me. She's a spoiled, jealous, nasty little . . ."

"We don't make accusations that reflect on the character of our passengers," the captain said stiffly. He nodded at the other two men and they seemed relieved to be able to leave the room. "For the present, because we try to keep this sort of thing quiet, Miss Sommers, I'm going to ask you to refrain from mixing with our passengers. Your protest may be wholly justified, but it would be too much to expect you not to talk about what's happened."

"I'm confined to my room? I'm under house arrest? Captain, if I'm guilty, I want to be arrested!" Jody did not know where she found the strength to challenge this man who seemed to inspire awe in every other member of the crew. "If you can't formally accuse me, you have no right to . . ."

"It's my unpleasant duty," Jody was told. The man seemed genuinely regretful. "This is the procedure, Miss Sommers, I hope you will cooperate. Innocent or guilty, I can't dismiss the matter. Or let you continue your activities as though nothing had happened."

He was telling Jody that she was not to leave the Whitecap deck. He explained that her meals would be brought to her cabin. And he was regretful that she would be unable to attend his farewell dinner. For a fleeting instant, Jody felt sorrier for the captain than she did for herself. But she could only listen numbly when he asked her not to "communicate" with the Westbrooks. How had he guessed that Jody's next move, after he left her alone, would have been to telephone Diane and demand that she tell the truth?

"Please understand that what I am asking of you is for your protection as well as for the consideration I must have for our passengers. We don't want this unpleasant incident to be discussed. We want no confrontations. You have my word that our security people will check everything you have said to me. In total confidence. But I can't make any accusation unless the passengers choose to press charges. And I'm sorry, Miss Sommers. On this night, which we all look forward to, it's particularly distressing for me to ask a new employee to . . . remain isolated. I truly have no recourse."

Nightmare, nightmare, nightmare! The captain was gone, and Jody stomped across the cabin, wanting to scream. What did Diane think she was going to accomplish? How rotten could anyone get? And why? Because she had been forcefully rejected by Neal? Because she was ravaged by jealousy? Jealousy about *what?*

Oh, the captain could talk about discretion and about keeping the matter a secret until it was thoroughly investigated. But did he suppose for one moment that Diane would not make the most of this carefully planned opportunity? There was no doubt in Jody's mind that Diane had slipped the brooch into her bag in a moment of impulsive vindictiveness. But wasn't it now a matter of Jody's word against that of the entire Westbrook family? *Scream!* She wanted to vent her outraged sense of justice, her searing frustration, in a loud, furious scream!

But the anger subsided, turning into pure misery. Jody looked into the full-length mirror. The butterfly dress, the gala evening, Neal's approving glances, perhaps . . . yes, perhaps even this dream job all of it suddenly erased, suddenly canceled! Jody threw herself across one of the beds, her fists pounding against the pillow. And, after a long, long time, the tears came; tears that should have relieved her anguish, but were only tears, after all. She found no relief. The nightmare persisted, unbelievable but horribly real.

What time was it when she heard the knocking on her door? Had she really fallen asleep? Cried until there was nothing else to do but fall asleep? Memory of what had happened flooded her mind as she made her way to the door. She opened it to see Terry Allin, dressed up in white formal wear. He stood outside her doorway for a few seconds, his blue eyes filled with pain. Then he moved forward and clasped Jody in a tight embrace.

She was crying again. Jody invited him in. "Are you sure you want to associate with me?"

Terry followed her into the cabin, closing the door behind him soundlessly. "Jody . . . Jody don't talk that way."

"You know what happened?"

Terry nodded solemnly. "I know. I wouldn't be able to believe it if I didn't know that trashy bunch. Honey, it's going to be all right. I know it's going to be all right."

"It's supposed to be kept discreet," Jody said bitterly. The yellow dress was wrinkled. Her makeup was probably smeared from crying. What a sight she must have presented to Terry! "I'm supposed to be staying here so that the nasty story doesn't spread all over the ship. But I'm sure everyone knows what happened by now. Who told you, Terry?"

"Shipboard grapevine," Terry acknowledged. He sat down on the edge of Jody's rumpled bed. "It infuriates me! I've told the captain exactly what I think. If she wasn't so busy, I'd haul that monstrous brat aside and I'd let her have it, too."

Jody sat down on the made-up bed opposite the doctor. "You don't believe . . ."

"Of course I don't believe what's being said," Terry said vehemently. "And I don't know how the story got out. I have my suspicions, but I don't really know."

"I can make a guess," Jody said. She looked at the travel alarm clock on her dresser, astounded to see that it was nearly eleven. "How did the dinner go?" she asked. "Weren't the decorations beautiful?"

Terry didn't care about the decorations. "I suffered through it. When I learned that you wouldn't be there, and why, I had all I could do to keep my promise to Prez. I'm always the . . . extra, available male. As you know."

Jody nodded. "Maybe you'd better get back to the party."

"I had to come and talk to you," he said. Jody could have sworn that there were tears in his eyes. "I wanted you to know that there's one person, one friend, who can't be made to believe . . ."

"I know." Jody thanked him for his faith in her.

Then, hurt by the fact that Terry had been the only person to come and express his trust in her, and wondering how many others had heard that she had stolen a valuable brooch from Elise Westbrook, she asked, "Have you talked to Prez?"

"He was very busy," Terry said. He sounded uneasy.

So Prez knew what had happened. But, concerned about his own job, not wanting to align himself with someone who might be dismissed and prosecuted for theft, he had chosen to be too preoccupied to give Jody his support.

"He's a weak little toady," Terry said. "Don't expect too much support from him."

Jody fought off the incipient tears. "And everyone else?"

"The ladies from California said they couldn't believe it."

"Couldn't? Or wouldn't?"

Terry's face looked flushed. "Jody . . . people aren't all as astute as I am. They don't know you as well as I do."

"What about . . . " Jody hesitated.

"Raincy? Neal Rainey?" Terry made a disgusted face. "I just saw him on the promenade . . . on the Neptune deck." It took Terry a long time before he said, "With *her*."

"Diane?"

"Yes. I always seem to be the one who brings you painful news, Jody. But you may as well know. They were drinking champagne, talking to nobody else, so wrapped up in conversation that they didn't even notice me when I went by. I wanted to push them both overboard."

"So, if anyone knows I'm confined to quarters, Neal must know. And he hasn't called to offer moral support. He hasn't done what you've done." Tears welled in Jody's eyes, then spilled over. She let them trickle across her cheeks. "You're the only friend I have on

175

this ship. And, Terry, what's going to happen? If they believe Diane, they have proof, don't they? They can prosecute me! I could go to prison as a common . . ."

Terry reached over to squeeze her hand. "Jody, don't. Please don't. And whatever happens, know that I believe in you. Believe in you and . . ."

Jody could have sworn that she knew what he would say next. And Terry Allin did not fail her. "Believe in you and love you," he said solemnly.

She reminded him that his presence was needed at the captain's party. And Jody assured him that she would be all right, that she was, in fact, very tired and would welcome being alone so that she could sleep.

As always, Terry probably knew better. But he left Jody with her dignity, promising to be in touch first thing in the morning.

Jody repaid his consideration by waiting until the doctor was well out of earshot before she broke into unconsolable sobs.

She had cried herself out, but her voice was raspy and raw from crying when she answered the ringing telephone about an hour later.

It was Neal. "Jody . . ."

She had started to cry again. "I can't talk to you now."

"Jody, there's something I have to talk to you about."

"Something you . . . discussed with Diane Westbrook?" She felt humiliated and embarrassed. Did he want to give her a lecture on honesty, or patronizingly offer his services as a criminal lawyer? Jody felt bloated from tears, not wanting to be seen, not wanting to face the added humiliation of having the man she loved offer to help her. "I don't want to talk to you," Jody cried. "I don't want to see you!"

"But I'm used to investigations and . . ."

She had slammed the receiver down, dissolving in

fitful sobs once more. When the telephone started to ring again, Jody yanked the phone jack out of the wall.

Later, she thought she heard someone knocking on her door, but that might only have been a dream, a part of the nightmare that had numbed her brain. When she was drained of tears, but not of her agony, Jody slept.

Chapter Fourteen

Jody awoke to the sound of someone knocking on her door. Someone *still* knocking? That couldn't be; morning light streamed in from the porthole. She glanced at her travel alarm, learning that it was nearly eight o'clock. The ship was in motion; they must be nearing Miami.

Now the sound that had awakened her had become a persistent pounding. Emotionally exhausted, the nightmare from which she could not awaken flooding over her, Jody called out in a groggy voice, "Who is it?"

"Jody?"

A pang of misery stabbed her as Jody recognized Neal's voice. She bit her lower lip, unable to respond.

"Jody, please let me in."

"I . . . I don't want to see you. I . . . can't."

"You've got to see me," Neal was insisting. "I want you to come up to the captain's quarters right away. And I want to talk to you."

Was she being summoned to an inquiry? Were they going to arrest her? "I don't need a lawyer," Jody shouted. She was crying again, but she got out of bed and walked closer to the locked door. "Last night I needed a friend. I don't need your services. I couldn't even . . . afford to hire you."

He was pounding again. "Will you please stop talking like a fool and let me in? We're wanted upstairs. Now."

"If the captain wants to see me, he'll let me know,"

Jody told him. "He knows where I am. I'm under house arrest."

"And you've probably pulled the phone out of the wall," Neal shouted. "I tried to call you all night. The captain's probably tried to call, too. Jody, will you please let me in?"

She had forgotten about the telephone. Jody leaned against the door, her legs shaking. She was so close to Neal; he was only inches away. And she wanted so desperately to be closer to him, to be in the arms of this man that she loved. But he was here to represent her in a criminal case—his specialty. If he had believed in her, loved her, he wouldn't have spent the evening with Diane Westbrook.

"Jody, you've got to let me in! I want to tell you what's happened."

Neal's persuasive manner, his strong voice, were suddenly irritating. Whatever he wanted, he sounded determined to have his way. "Look, everything's going to be all right. I'll go upstairs with you, and it's all going to be all right."

Jody didn't move from the door. She let the bitter tears roll down her face. It wasn't going to be "all right." No matter what happened, even if she was able to clear herself, she would not forget the pain of Neal's desertion. He had been with Diane when he must have known Jody was sobbing herself to sleep. And all of the clever legal techniques he might use would not erase the fact that he must have believed her to be guilty of theft. This man, who had held her close and showered her with kisses, would never convince her that everything was going to be "all right."

She heard Neal make an exasperated sound. "I wanted to talk to you before we went up," he said. "But if you won't do that, meet me outside the captain's quarters in ten minutes."

"I'm not sure I'm . . . even supposed to leave my . . ."

"That's an order!" Neal roared. "Ten minutes, Jody. Be there!"

He didn't explain whether the order had come from the captain or was his own. Then he was gone, Jody knew. She crossed the room, catching a glimpse of herself in the dressing table mirror. She was disgusted with herself for having fallen asleep in the beautiful chiffon dress; it looked limp and bedraggled. There was a circle of mascara under one eye and her face was puffy from crying. And she was *still* crying; she felt as though the tears would never stop.

Always before, when she got herself ready for a meeting with Neal, her heart beat excitedly with anticipation. It was hammering now, as Jody prepared herself for whatever inquisition she would have to face, but there was another reason for that erratic tattoo. When she repeated the truth, would Neal believe her? Probably not. If he thought she was innocent, he wouldn't think she needed his services. And she didn't want him to see her the way she looked now, didn't want him to be a witness to her anguish.

A shower, fresh makeup and a change of clothes helped Jody's appearance but did little to lift her spirits. She was nervous and frightened, dreading the ordeal of having to tell her story again. And she was afraid that she wouldn't be able to control her tears; if she broke down and cried like a baby, her humiliation would be complete.

It was a full fifteen minutes before Jody got to the deck that housed the captain's living quarters, chart room and private office. Neal was waiting for her, glancing at his watch impatiently as Jody approached. When he saw her, Neal extended his hands. "Good morning, Jody. We won't have time to talk, I'm afraid. We're late now."

"I don't know what there is to talk about," Jody said. Her voice quavered, but she kept her head up high, ignoring Neal's outstretched arms. He took her hands in his, nevertheless, pressing them firmly. "I told you," Jody went on, "that I can't afford a . . . celebrated trial lawyer. I've told the truth, and that ought to be enough."

"Jody, I'm not here as your attorney. I'm here as your friend. And as a witness."

"Witness? You weren't around when . . ."

"I know that. And I'm going to present hearsay testimony that wouldn't stand up in any court. But I want you to know that I'm on your side. I believed you were innocent even before I got Diane's admission."

"Admission?"

"We're late," Neal said. "We'd better get inside."

Neal opened the door to reveal a long conference table. She was shocked to see not only the captain and the security man and the steward who had searched her cabin, but all three of the Westbrooks. Evidently they were going to press charges. Jody's lungs felt airless. Maybe she *would* need a lawyer. She let Neal guide her to a chair, silently praying that she would not start crying again.

The captain and his crew members rose and then sat down again as Jody was seated. Neal took the chair next to hers. Dalton and Diane did not look in her direction. Elise nodded.

Then, the captain was saying, "Mr. Westbrook . . . Mrs. Westbrook, I've told you what Mr. Rainey told me about your daughter's admission to him late last night."

Dalton banged his fist on the table. "He got her drunk on champagne! He's a smart lawyer! Diane probably didn't even know what she was saying." He glared at Neal. "*If* she said anything at all. My daughter wouldn't do a thing like that. Why would she?"

"Because of an incident that I'd rather not remind you of, Mr. Westbrook." Neal's tone was patient but firm. Even under these circumstances he didn't reveal that he had virtually thrown Diane out of his room.

"And because Diane knows that I have a . . . strong personal interest in Jody Sommers." Neal paused, then went on quietly. "Last night, when I heard the story, I'll admit that I made it a point to gain Diane's confidence. I'll admit that I used every investigative technique, every nuance of cross-examination that's known to me. And I'll also admit that Diane had been drinking heavily. When she told me that she'd placed that brooch in Miss Sommers' handbag, she was giggling. as though she had done something terribly clever."

Dalton leaped to his feet. "You get a nineteen-year-old kid intoxicated and you. . . ."

"She had managed to do that quite on her own," Neal said calmly. "A good hour before I heard about the alleged theft."

"That's not true, is it, baby?" Dalton laid a hand on his daughter's shoulder. "You tell these people exactly what you told me!"

Diane closed her eyes. She looked as though she might be ill and she made no response.

"Please be seated, Mr. Westbrook," the captain said. "We've all heard your daughter's testimony."

Turning to Neal, the captain said, "Mr. Rainey, I certainly appreciate your concern in behalf of one of our staff members. We're very proud of the integrity of our crew. We've never had an unfortunate incident like this before, and, frankly, you've presented me with a case that would take a King Solomon to decide. I have your word and the word of one of our passengers as to what was actually said last night. Conflicting stories. And . . . there is the unfortunate circumstantial evidence."

Neal nodded grimly. "I understand, Captain."

Looking from one participant to the next, the captain was obviously distressed. He wanted to be fair, Jody guessed. He wanted to be just. But Neal's admission that he had deliberately trapped Diane Westbrook into a "confession," which she now denied, could hardly exonerate a new employee in whose possession the expensive brooch had been found. "I'm afraid that under the circumstances," the captain went on in a somber tone, "I have no choice but to . . ."

"I want to say something!"

The startling, emotion-wracked sentence brought everyone's attention to Elise Westbrook.

"I want to say something," she repeated. She looked determined and when the captain invited her to speak, Elise squared her shoulders and said, "This isn't the first time."

"Elise, you're turning on your own . . ."

Dalton's fury was cut off by his wife's anguished cry. "Do you have any idea . . . how much it hurts me to say what I'm going to say? *Any* idea of how painful it is for me to say this about my own child?" Elise lowered her head, her whole body trembling. Diane didn't look up at her mother. She sat tight-lipped, staring at the tabletop, her eyes narrowed.

"It's not the first time," Elise repeated. Her voice dropped down to a hoarse whisper. "There was the science teacher at Miss Pettigrew's school. Diane was wild about him. He was going with one of the other teachers. And there were . . . seven hundred dollars from the Nature Club Fund that were missing. They found the money in Miss Larrimer's room. She lost her job. Her young man never spoke to her again. And Diane knew too many details about how that money got where they found it. She slipped up once, talking about it, and I knew." Elise swallowed hard. "Then at that other school in Switzerland . . ."

Elise went on, her voice barely audible. Diane didn't offer any protest. Jody glanced across the table to see that Diane's hands were shaking, but there was no sign of emotion on that beautiful face. Her mother stopped several times to daub at her eyes with a soggy handkerchief, but she went on resolutely, detailing incidents in which Diane had resolved her jealous frustrations by making a patsy, even a criminal, of anyone who stood in the way of her current romantic whim. Dalton was no longer protesting. He sat shaking his head from side to side, as though he couldn't believe that his wife would reveal the sordid stories about their only child.

It was too much for Elise. She closed her eyes for a moment and was silent. Then she said, "And we didn't help her, did we, Dalton? We love Diane, but we didn't help her to change. You . . . we always swept it all under the carpet and pretended that nothing was wrong." Elise turned to her daughter. "Do you understand why I was the . . . the 'mean mother,' Diane? Because you're my little girl, too. And I love you. I love you so much. . . . I didn't want this to ever happen again."

Were Dalton's eyes misted over? It seemed so to Jody. And although it was doubtful that Diane had ever shed tears, except in childish temper tantrums, she couldn't help being touched by her mother's heartbreak. Only an iceberg would not have been affected.

The captain got to his feet. The two crew members followed suit. "I think Miss Sommers is due for an apology," he said. "From all of us. And I think, since the brooch is back in your possession, Mrs. Westbrook . . ."

It was over. The Westbrooks agreed that no charges would be pressed. Diane's eyes didn't meet Jody's as she muttered a sullen, "I'm sorry."

As the Westbrooks filed out of the room, Dalton gave Neal a surly look, but he looked ashamed. Ashamed and depressed and, just possibly, Jody hoped, beginning to wonder if this humiliation would have been avoided if he had not pampered his daughter with his misguided interpretation of love.

Elise stopped for just a moment as she passed Jody. She reached out to press Jody's hand. "Thank you," she said softly. "For giving me the . . . strength to do that after all these years. And for . . . for being my friend."

The captain echoed Diane's apology to Jody and he thanked Neal for his concern. When she reached the fresh-aired sanity of the deck, Jody felt as though she had been run through an old-fashioned wringer.

Neal linked his arm through Jody's as they walked. "I'm not for having breakfast with all those people in the dining room," he said. "What about the top deck, Jody? Just the two of us?" .

Why did she hesitate? She owed him her most profound gratitude. Still, a fear that she loved him too much and could still be hurt by him brought a lame excuse to Jody's lips. "I don't know. Prez probably has work for me to do." It was the weakest alibi imaginable: not minutes ago Jody wasn't even thinking of herself as an employee.

"I'll be leaving the ship in a few hours," Neal said as they walked along the promenade deck." "I'd like to have some time alone with you."

"I felt the same way last night," Jody said.

"I tried to reach you after I'd gotten what I wanted out of Diane. Earlier, I didn't think you'd welcome any more company." There was a terse edge to the way Neal spoke.

"More company?"

"I knew Dr. Allin had gone to your room."

"Of course he came to my room," Jody responded. "He's my friend."

Neal's tone was suddenly scathing. "Well, thank you, Miss Sommers!"

"I don't mean to sound ungrateful for . . . " Jody looked at Neal's face, seeing its handsome perfection marred by a furious scowl. "I appreciate what you've done for me and . . ."

"I don't want your pitiful gratitude," Neal yelled. "I did an atrociously unprofessional thing. My colleagues would laugh at my pitiful 'testimony.'"

"Still, you tried," Jody said.

"Yes, I tried! I was determined to get Diane to slip up and admit that she tried to frame you. When I did, I wanted nothing more than to tell you about that. But you had another shoulder to lean on." Neal released his breath angrily. "I can't blame you. I'll be leaving the ship, flying back to San Francisco. I let you know that I'm not into . . . falling in love with *any* woman. How can I fault you for cultivating a man who's a permanent fixture aboard this ship? You'll need somebody to squire you around when I'm gone." Neal's face had become a glowering mask. "And you'll have Dr. Allin's suite to rendezvous in."

Jody's nerves had been scraped raw. "What right do you have to say that to me? Haven't I been through enough? You have absolutely no right to be . . . " Jody spun away from Neal, too emotionally worn out to go on with the senseless discussion. "What right do you have . . ."

"To be jealous?" Neal had finished the sentence for her.

Jody was hurrying toward the nearest elevator when Neal's words stopped her. He shouted them, firmly, positively, loud enough for every startled passenger on the deck to hear: "I have every right to be jealous! I love you! Did you hear what I just said, Jody? *I love you!*"

Jody stopped short. Then she turned around slowly. She was going to be crying again in another instant and she had cried enough.

There were five or six yards between them, but their eyes met, closing the distance, drawing them together. And then Jody was tumbling forward into Neal's arms, echoing his words, "I love *you!* Oh, Neal, I'm so afraid. You're so far beyond what I'd ever hoped for myself but, heaven help me, I love you, too. I love you with all my heart!"

There was no romantic moonlit path over the sea.

The morning sun danced on the whitecaps and revealed a dazzling shoreline as the *Caribe Queen* approached Miami. But she was safe and warm in Neal's strong arms, and, oblivious to the other passengers, he was kissing her, stopping to brush the tears from her face with his hand and then kissing her again, holding her as though he would never let her go.

"I've been so afraid of love," Neal murmured against Jody's ear. "But I can't fight it anymore. I need you. I love you and I trust you. Tell me you need me, too."

Jody didn't reply with words. Clinging to that powerful, protective body, she told Neal all that he wanted to know.

"My flight leaves Miami at four thirty," Neal said as he lifted his lips from Jody's.

"Yes." A hard lump had risen in Jody's throat. "Please stay aboard, Neal. Until the very last minute."

"I'll stay long enough to help you pack," he said.

Jody looked up at him, the question in her eyes.

"You don't owe Prez MacCauley two weeks' notice. When he said, last night, that he didn't doubt your innocence, the hypocrisy could have been cut with a knife. You don't need him or this job or anything, anyone else but me."

A moonlit path on the Caribbean would have created a more appropriate setting for what Neal said next. But here, in the brilliant morning sunlight, amid the bustle of waiters and passengers, and with the blare of a welcoming brass band on the shore, he said, "I want you to marry me, Jody. I want to take care of you for the rest of my life. Please, darling. Say good-bye to your nice doctor friend. Tell Mr. MacCauley that you'd rather be Mrs. Rainey than his assistant. Tell me to cancel my flight and wait for you if you can't pack fast enough. We'll stop over to see if your folks approve of me. Just tell me we're going to be together for the rest of our lives!"

Neal had a way of being strong and sincere and

persuasive. A brilliant attorney had to be. But this was one case he didn't have to plead. Jody's eyes were misty, but the tears that had risen in her eyes were tears of joy. She slipped her hand into Neal's, and together they walked toward the cruise director's office.

"Your flight is supposed to leave when, darling?"

"Whenever you're ready. My ticket says four thirty."

Jody's fingers tightened around Neal's, pressing them tightly. "If I hurry—say good-bye to Terry, give Prez my notice and toss my clothes into my luggage—I think, my dearest, that I could be ready before three."

IT'S YOUR OWN SPECIAL TIME

Contemporary romances for today's women.
Each month, six very special love stories will be yours
from SILHOUETTE. Look for them wherever books are sold
or order now from the coupon below.

$1.50 each

Hampson	☐ 1 ☐ 4 ☐ 16 ☐ 27 ☐ 28 ☐ 40 ☐ 52 ☐ 64 ☐ 94	Browning	☐ 12 ☐ 38 ☐ 53 ☐ 73 ☐ 93
Stanford	☐ 6 ☐ 25 ☐ 35 ☐ 46 ☐ 58 ☐ 88	Michaels	☐ 15 ☐ 32 ☐ 61 ☐ 87
		John	☐ 17 ☐ 34 ☐ 57 ☐ 85
Hastings	☐ 13 ☐ 26 ☐ 44 ☐ 67	Beckman	☐ 8 ☐ 37 ☐ 54 ☐ 72 ☐ 96
Vitek	☐ 33 ☐ 47 ☐ 66 ☐ 84		

$1.50 each

☐ 3 Powers	☐ 29 Wildman	☐ 56 Trent	☐ 79 Halldorson
☐ 5 Goforth	☐ 30 Dixon	☐ 59 Vernon	☐ 80 Stephens
☐ 7 Lewis	☐ 31 Halldorson	☐ 60 Hill	☐ 81 Roberts
☐ 9 Wilson	☐ 36 McKay	☐ 62 Hallston	☐ 82 Dailey
☐ 10 Caine	☐ 39 Sinclair	☐ 63 Brent	☐ 83 Hallston
☐ 11 Vernon	☐ 41 Owen	☐ 69 St. George	☐ 86 Adams
☐ 14 Oliver	☐ 42 Powers	☐ 70 Afton Bonds	☐ 89 James
☐ 19 Thornton	☐ 43 Robb	☐ 71 Ripy	☐ 90 Major
☐ 20 Fulford	☐ 45 Carroll	☐ 74 Trent	☐ 92 McKay
☐ 21 Richards	☐ 48 Wildman	☐ 75 Carroll	☐ 95 Wisdom
☐ 22 Stephens	☐ 49 Wisdom	☐ 76 Hardy	☐ 97 Clay
☐ 23 Edwards	☐ 50 Scott	☐ 77 Cork	☐ 98 St. George
☐ 24 Healy	☐ 55 Ladame	☐ 78 Oliver	☐ 99 Camp

$1.75 each

☐ 100 Stanford	☐ 104 Vitek	☐ 108 Hampson	☐ 112 Stanford
☐ 101 Hardy	☐ 105 Eden	☐ 109 Vernon	☐ 113 Browning
☐ 102 Hastings	☐ 106 Dailey	☐ 110 Trent	☐ 114 Michaels
☐ 103 Cork	☐ 107 Bright	☐ 111 South	☐ 115 John
	☐ 116 Lindley	☐ 117 Scott	

Introducing
First Love from Silhouette

Romances for teenage girls to build their dreams on.

They're wholesome, fulfilling, supportive novels about every young girl's dreams. Filled with the challenges, excitement—and responsibilities—of love's first blush, *First Love* paperbacks prepare young adults to stand at the threshold of maturity with confidence and composure.

Introduce your daughter, or some young friend to the *First Love* series by giving her a one-year subscription to these romantic originals, written by leading authors. She'll receive two NEW $1.75 romances each month, a total of 24 books a year. Send in your coupon now. **There's nothing quite as special as a First Love.**

Silhouette Romance

15-Day Free Trial Offer
6 Silhouette Romances

6 Silhouette Romances, free for 15 days! We'll send
you 6 new Silhouette Romances to keep for 15 days, absolutely
free! If you decide not to keep them, send them back to us.
You pay nothing.

Free Home Delivery. But if you enjoy them as much as we
think you will, keep them by paying the invoice enclosed with
your free trial shipment. We'll pay all shipping and handling
charges. You get the convenience of Home Delivery and we
pay the postage and handling charge each month.

Don't miss a copy. The Silhouette Book Club is the way
to make sure you'll be able to receive every new romance we
publish before they're sold out. There is no minimum number
of books to buy and you can cancel at any time.

This offer expires June 30, 1982